LOVE and the Bay Street Bingo Players

LOVE and the Bay Street Bingo Players

As Told by
Ferdinand Daniel Swasont to
John D. Frankel

THE FINAL VOLUME OF A TWO-PART TRILOGY

ISBN 978-1-988360-01-0 (paperback)
ISBN 978-1-988360-02-7 (ePUB)
ISBN 978-1-988360-03-4 (ePDF)

Note for librarians: a Cataloguing in Publication record for
this book is available from Library and Archives Canada at
www.collectionscanada.ca/amicus/index-e.html.

Editor: Michael Carroll
Book design: Daniel Crack, Kinetics Design, kdbooks.ca
linkedin.com/in/kdbooks

Cover photos:
Buildings: shutterstock.com., phoelixDE, Image ID: 453211969
Pedestrians on Bay Street:
commons.wikimedia.org/wiki/File:Pedestrians_on_Bay_Street.jpg

To my Bevy, once again and always

Full, True, and Plain Disclosure

Some readers (two to be exact) of *The Independent Republic of Harvey Markson* claimed they were intrigued by Zygmunt Adams, one of the main characters of that opus. Even Harvey Markson agreed there was a story there. He felt it should be written with all the respect a memorial deserves.

But the production of *The Republic* (the novel's short name, though scooped by Plato twenty-four hundred years earlier) taught Harvey two things: only half-crazed individuals write books. The planet produces a million or two new books each year, he argued, why in the world would it need one more? Second, though he agreed to be interviewed and to forward all relevant emails, Harvey thought the most intelligence-deprived activity next to writing a book was to undertake to find a publisher for one.

So I stepped in.

1. I am an experienced writer. When I finally passed the exam to become a licensed financial adviser, my brother asked me to take over the writing of our family company's newsletter – *Swasont Brothers' & Mayham's Monthly Investment Insights*. I did that for twelve years and gained a great deal of authorial experience. But, because I acted at the same time as a commissioned salesman (a "registered representative") in the investment business, some people claimed I was somewhat loose with facts.

At least that was the way sympathetic readers put it. The less sensitive ones, including a few former clients, accused me of being a consummate bullshitter. To be frank, sometimes in the investment world one needs to speculate on situations. Although I am a thorough researcher and did dozens and dozens of interviews to put Zyg's story together here, I admit that at times I had to fill in gaps that my research could not possibly have unearthed. I am not the first writer in history to do that, believe me.

2. Furthermore, in the interests of full disclosure, I should also point out that there were rumours freighted about, especially by (not to name names) my ex-sister-in-law, that I had sought the help of a sex therapist, or more precisely, to use her expression, that I had problems with my hydraulics. Allow me to refute that accusation here and now. Not common knowledge at the time was the fact that I supported a lap dancer I met at a night class in ethics (a subject I knew little about having spent my working life in the investment business). I supported her through her divinity studies right up until she moved away to become the pastor of a small parish outside Ottawa.

Today, too many relationships turn out to be nothing more than temporary arrangements driven into by here-today-gone-tomorrow lust. For one thing, until Swasont Brothers & Mayham was once again on sound financial footing, I did not want the expense, complications, encumbrances, or anguish of the typical urban male/female relationship you find today. It's as simple as that. While Zyg was known in many quarters as the Mr. WD-40 of the Bar-and-Squeaky-Bed Set, accusations of envy on my part, let me assure you, would be entirely unfounded.

With those two possibilities – journalistic tendencies and sexual envy – dealt with openly and frankly, for the sake of emphasis let me add a disclaimer. In fairness, most of the wording comes from the prospectus of the latest "initial public offering" (an expression created to replace "new issue" and make things clearer for the average investor) brought to market by the Federal Wealth and Great Trust Company, a division of the Federal Financial Group of Canada:

Some of what you read may not jibe with reality or with other reports of the same events. Some gaps in the research, however diligent, might be filled in for the sake of narrative continuity. It is a good idea, if not more, to double-check all references and dates before quoting the material herein. Past performance is no guarantee of future performance.

Note: While good performance in investing offers no assurance whatsoever of repetition in the future, many studies suggest poor performance tends to persist, much like a character flaw.

OCTOBER 2010
FERDINAND DANIEL SWASONT

1

Explosive Breaking News

2003

Like a one-eyed king, the big clock in the tower of the Old City Hall, the flower beds below freshly turned, peered down lower Bay Street between the tall bank buildings as if to keep a watch on things. Its view of the harbour was blocked by an ugly raised expressway, the on and off ramps clogged all day long, mostly with people coming from or going to the city's financial district.

Of late, life had not been kind to that district – "The Street," as those who work there like to call it – which had suffered the aftermath of the high-tech binge at the end of the twentieth century. Not kind at all. Just a block south of the clock tower, though, the hint of spring and the recent sandblast to restore the yellow brick facade of the thirty-two-storey office building at 370 Bay suggested one of the tenants might get a new lease on life.

And though they objected, and very vigorously, to the size of the rent increase that went along with their new lease, still, the tenants of the fourth floor of 370 felt a solution to their recent problems was close at hand. The corporate brochure referred to the fourth floor as "The Head Office of IED Securities Inc., one of Canada's most prestigious investment houses since 1969."

Mind you, the Winnipeg branch of IED had a slightly different description for those premises. When Toronto phoned in, the speaker system would announce something like "Mr. Bennett, Clownhaven on line two for you, sir."

Wilfred Cross Bennett, an old classmate of mine from boarding school, was in charge of the Winnipeg office. He had just returned from two weeks of golf in Phoenix, Arizona, and had come in an hour early before everybody that particular Monday morning to catch up on his emails. He scrolled down through the dozens and dozens of messages that awaited him, deleting one after the other, many unread (stopping only – knowing him – for discount offers on libido boosters and enlargement pills), until his cursor highlighted the subject "Welcome Our New President." That one he read. That one he read word for word.

"Jesus Christ!" Cross blurted out with not a soul around to hear. Then he reread the message, all 58 kilobytes, and repeated those same words, this time a little slower and a little louder. Next he shouted in short, chopped syllables, "I mean, Jee-sus. Jee-sus Kee–riced!" rotating his freshly tanned head from side to side, eyelids clamped shut over his small brown eyes, one hand massaging his square moustache. "Has everybody down there gone stark-raving goddamn nuts? I mean, Zyg Adams? Just what we need – a sex fiend for president! That's the guy who'll save us? Are you kidding me? Jee-sus! I mean, for the love of God, that little four-eyed fornicator has slipped into more beds than a worn-out bedpan. Are we really that goddamn desperate?"

Cross then looked away from his computer. "You know what I think? I think sooner or later this whole goddamn company is going to blow up," he informed the empty office.

2
A Bit of a Challenge

One school of thought argued that the wording "one of Canada's most prestigious investment dealers since 1969" implied IED Securities Inc. had been around long before that and only became prestigious in 1969. That, however, was actually the year the company was founded. Two old Toronto firms with old Toronto names that no longer carried any weight – Irwin & Co. and Elsworth-Densmore – merged, the new partnership settling for the name "IED." In case something went wrong, as it so often had, how much better to drag letters of the alphabet through the mud than old Toronto names once again.

Over the next three decades, like the inscrutable movements of stock prices, IED journeyed through many ups and many downs, but unlike most markets, through many more downs than ups. In 1974, with an oil embargo and the Dow Jones Index of U.S. stocks hitting what turned out to be a low point unmatched in the decades that followed, partners begrudgingly had to throw in capital to keep the proud ship afloat. In early May of 1980, two weeks before the Province of Quebec held a referendum on whether or not to separate from the rest of Canada, the Montreal partners had had enough and closed down their office having guessed, incorrectly, that *les séparatistes* would win the day.

Then, in 1981, after just three years in business, the Calgary office closed up shop when the oil business in Alberta, in the words of *The World of Finance*, "plunged" into some lean years, very lean, indeed. Three members of the Calgary staff opened a Vancouver branch, but the timing, always difficult to get quite right, was definitely quite wrong. Then, in 1986, cirrhosis of the liver and concomitant hepatitis claimed the life of the eldest founder, Mr. A.A. Irwin. A year later the stock market took so severe a drop – 22.6 percent in one day – that the two remaining founders, Messieurs Ellsworth and Densmore, threw in the towel. They foresaw nothing except bleak times ahead for the stock market, times as bleak as the Great Depression, especially Mr. Densmore, an economics major at university. So the two men sold their interests and disappeared.

By then only the head office in Toronto and a branch office in Winnipeg existed. More precisely, co-existed.

In its history, even at its most successful, IED was never what you would call a significant or important brokerage house. Any attempt to make a significant increase in its size and importance, an astute investor would take as a sure sign – "a leading indicator" – that the stock market was about to tumble, or as they say on The Street, head south, very south. After every expansion, a bloodbath followed. Then, and only then, wounded and oozing red ink, would IED slim down to its fighting weight of about seventy-three people, twenty-three of whom held the title of vice-president or better. Of those twenty-three, sixteen had no executive responsibility at all, their titles awarded solely for marketing purposes.

In 1989, IED's ad agency translated that rich history into a corporate symbol – a fluted Doric column – to imply stability. (Within a day, the new logo became known throughout the company as "The Shaft.") To go along with that logo, the tag line underneath the IED Securities Inc. name on all letterhead and envelopes and all forms, all business cards, on the corporate brochure, and in all its newspaper ads, and later, on its website read: "Stability. Integrity. Compactness."

Naturally, what appealed most to the two new major shareholders was the compactness. Though small, IED had most of the components of the much larger, bank-owned brokerage houses. For Sherwin Chable, chairman, CEO, and president, and his cousin, Martin Chable, vice-chairman, IED's configuration suited them to a T. Their expertise lay in helping small technology, biotechnology, and mining companies share with the public the rewards of nearly new ventures.

It had a comfortable and attractive reception area where several reproductions of Cornelius Krieghoff's lush winter scenes played off against the Wedgwood blue walls and the dark blue broadloom, somewhat time-worn in front of the receptionist's desk. At the centre of the room, draped in beaded-glass strands, hung a château-sized chandelier, all but a six or seven of its dozens of little bulbs glowing. A set of dark mahogany-stained doors opened into a boardroom, the walls proudly bearing the photo portraits of the three glum-faced founders. The large mahogany table could seat all of IED's top executives and quite a few vice-presidents for sales meetings. The harsh glare of the overhead lights, much like you'd expect in a police interrogation room, could be lowered for meetings with clients or left bright, should a vice-president get engaged, for an all-night crap game.

The other door in the reception area opened onto a long corridor. On the left was a pair of glass doors – the entrance to the executive suite – which could only be opened by a plastic ID card or when one of the administrative assistants inside pushed a button. A little farther along and on the opposite wall hung a large needlepoint rendition of the Great Wall of China, meant to assure the world that the reams of confidential information held behind in the investment banking department remained … confidential. Rumour had it, though, that in nearby bars after work, or on suburban golf courses during weekends, cracks sometimes formed in The Wall.

Farther along the corridor was the research department of Skly Cszymorska (pronounced *skly cszymor-ska*, as the welcome-on-board memo clarified) and his two research analysts. And beyond Skly's office lay a great hall with two long rows of desks, separated by a shoulder-high partition, which held the work desks of IED's thirty-two registered representatives. Most often they were called "reps" (interchangeably called "The Producers"), the people who dealt with the customers (interchangeably referred to as clients). The room constantly buzzed with phone chatter and outbursts of laughter, all overseen from a glass-walled office by the darting eyes of Don-Phil de Vita, senior vice-president of sales.

Beyond the desks of the reps on the far side of the hall sat the back-to-back desks of the two equity traders, as well as that of the head (and only) bond trader (Cross Bennett's job in the early 1980s).

Next to the men's toilet sat the "Back Office." Its job was to handle all the paperwork the reps created and to make sure of adherence to the infinite number of regulations. The air smelled stale. The yellow walls had faded into a dirty-water grey. The hand-me-down desks, chipped and scratched, looked ready for pickup any day by the Salvation Army. That department – administration and compliance – consisted of two tiny offices and five cubicles, the staff all crammed together as snugly and gloomily as the contents of a sardine can, not a vice-president in the lot.

In spite of the predictions made by the two founding fathers when they sold their interests in late 1987, stock prices did begin to rise. And despite the "Housing Bubble of 1989," the U.S. Savings and Loan Crisis of '89, the Kuwaiti Crisis of 1990, the Asian Currency Crisis of 1997, and the Russian Financial Crisis of 1998, stock prices moved up and up. And IED customer-clients bought up large chunks of every initial public offering the company brought to market. By 1999, wealthier than they ever dreamed they'd be, the majority shareholders of IED, both men in their late fifties, took most of their profits "off the table" in the form of bonuses, dividends, stock buybacks, and the sale of shares to their partners, then retired to Panama. For reasons, both claimed, of health.

Winnipeg's diagnosis? A chronic allergy to taxes.

Nothing at all seemed wrong with the cousin, Martin, who took Pilates classes three times a week. And although Sherwin carried thirty pounds of excess weight, he never missed a weekend of skiing in winter. His only visible ailment came from an accident at Snowbird, Utah, when a member of the Church of Jesus Christ of Latter-day Saints skied into him. He called the limp his "Mormon Knee" and complained about it incessantly to anyone who would listen.

The title of chief executive officer of IED then fell upon the broad shoulders of Robert Wiseman Little, at one time a lumbering all-star right guard for a small college in the Maritimes. He graduated with average grades (very average) in the late 1970s, and for the next two decades lumbered along as a broker-without-distinction. Then, suddenly, with the final up-wave of the markets in the late 1990s, he caught on to the game. For three years straight, he "produced" more than a million and a half dollars in commissions (47 percent of which he got to keep before taxes). He did that by trading clients in and out of stocks as the market made its jagged ascent toward the year 2000, many of the stocks those freshly minted by the Chables and their Street confreres such as the highly influential Federal Wealth and Great Trust Co. owned by one of the big five banks.

For the first two years as a top salesman and the contributor of hundreds of thousands of dollars to company revenues, "Big Bobby" Little was presented, out of a sense of gratitude, with tickets to the opening Toronto Blue Jays baseball game. By the third year, though, the firm had no choice but to recognize his efforts. To his title of vice-president was added that of chief equity strategist. Not five days later, the producer of *This Week in Capital Markets*, its theme song James Carlie White's melodic "Cracked Pots Cantata" (in C major), phoned with an invitation to appear on the show.

And right after that appearance, a call came in from Toby Williams from *Today's Business*. Toby wrote a tough-minded column, highly critical of the financial industry and its adamant refusal to put in writing, in any place other than its advertising, that the client's interest came first. The column, entitled "Frequently Unanswered Questions," was referred to by The Street by its acronym, "FUQs," pronounced *few-Qs*, or more commonly, as *fuh-Qs*.

Other nightly business news programs, both television and radio, began to invite Mr. Little to pass on his investment wisdom. Hardly a week went by in those days when one writer or another from the business media did not seek out the views of IED's chief equity strategist for the "quotes" needed to complete their columns. And, of course, *The World of Finance*'s good old Halvert Tulvin started to call regularly on the lookout as always for gossip droppings for his "Goings-On" column, opening with the standard inquiry used by all top-notch investigative journalists these days: "Anybody new in the doo-doo?"

1999

The tight-fisted Chables left the day-to-day scene to become "The Gentlemen of Panama," as Winnipeg referred to them. Chairman Chable's outsized office, the sole exception to IED's core value of compactness, referred to by Winnipeg as "The Ballroom"(any request from there for co-operation as "a dance invitation"), fell to Big Bobby just as the twentieth century breathed its last few weeks.

One bit of esoteric financial theory claims you'd need at least sixteen years to determine with reasonable certainty whether the performance, or track record, of an investment manager, whom financial people prefer to call a "money manager," was due to innate skill or to sheer luck.

Whichever was at play for him in the late 1990s – luck or skill – it vanished almost the moment Big Bobby Little sat down behind the king-sized, blond-maple desk in his new office with its magnificent view of the bank building next door. The world for Big Bobby, however, turned rough. Very, very rough. In fact, a full-scale storm broke out in the markets over the following months. Clients, who relied on common sense rather than statistical theory, took less than sixteen years to conclude that whatever was at play in Big Bobby's success, it was definitely not skill.

As the stock market began its rapid descent in the early days of the new millennium, so, too, did the value of the portfolios of IED's clients, often with greater velocity. Within eighteen months, millions and millions of dollars of client wealth disappeared from the face of the earth. From habits formed over the previous two decades when markets just kept going up and up, IED's reps/producers advised clients/customers to take advantage of market dips to buy this or that stock at a "bargain" price.

"Our research people think we'll never see Pluman's Funeral Homes at this price again in our lifetimes. Don't forget, people die every day." That was the kind of argument you'd hear – every day – from the work desks at IED Unfortunately, IED's clients discovered that in this new century many "buying opportunities" turned out not to be bargains at all. Quite the opposite. And in the case of Pluman's Funeral Homes, for example, it turned out that, yes, true enough, people were dying every day, but some of the people still living changed the accounting rules.

Nobody at IED had foreseen for a moment the issuance of Financial Accounting Standards Board Bulletin #1407-Q-(ii)b, which stated that funeral homes could no longer book so-called "pre-need" sales as current revenue. Lest the prospective client had a change of heart and switched to another supplier before the actual "need" for a funeral arose, the new rules stated that enterprises in the "death-care" industry could no longer count "pre-need" sales immediately as revenue. That change alone took away a quarter of the annual revenue declared by Pluman's. Its board of directors eliminated the fifty-cent dividend. And the stock price shrank quickly and efficiently and quite in keeping with financial theory (see E. Fama, "The Behaviour of Stock Market Prices," *The Journal of Business* 38, no. 1 [January 1965]: 34–105).

2002

"Hey, Big Bobby, a couple of years back you talked me into a thousand shares of Pluman's when it came on the market at twenty-four, remember?" a long-time client inquired.

"I don't remember exactly. Was it twenty-four?"

"And I told you Gerry Pluman wouldn't sell his company for anything other than top dollar. Well, I can't get four bucks for the shit today. So, like, tell me this, Mr. Smarty-President, where the hell did my twenty grand go?"

Not an unfair question. Perhaps a good "FUQs" question for Toby Williams over at *Today's Business*. When somebody's willing to pay you $24 a share one month and not a nickel more than $4 the next, where does that $20 difference go?

The incumbent CEO and president of IED hesitated for a moment, cupped a hand to his chin, and replied, "Into thin air, I guess, Doctor."

That was just one example. There were all kinds of similar calamities when investors decided out of the blue that a great idea, a snappy name, and no revenue were not sufficient conditions for a company's future profitability, especially start-up dot-coms run by children just out of high school. Rethinking such as that resulted in price drops as drastic as those of the shares of Pluman's Funeral Homes Inc.

As company after company went out of business and the price of their shares hit bottom, you could almost hear that deadly thump as they fell to earth.

The markets plunged and kept falling until every bit of optimism was squeezed out of the participants (the very best time, claimed Sir John Templeton, to invest). From the high-water mark, not considering money withdrawn, many of the accounts at IED dropped 40 percent, some even more. Many who had been talked into borrowing money in the hope of even greater gains would likely have lost all of his or her capital, perhaps even some they didn't have. Out of IED's eight thousand clients, not even a half dozen blamed the stock market itself for this catastrophic outcome. A few blamed their own indecisiveness. But by far the majority felt IED Securities Inc. was negligent. Some even said criminally negligent.

"What the hell does IED stand for? Investable explosive devices?" one enraged client is said to have shrieked over the phone with such volume you'd think she was on the fourth floor of 370 Bay and not, as always at that time of year, in her condo on Longboat Key next to Sarasota, Florida.

Like a contagion, the anger spread. Customers and/or clients phoned the various regulators – the OSC, CSA, MFDA, IIROC, OSFI, FISCO, RCMP, every organization except Interpol (not listed in the phone book) – claiming gross misrepresentation. Such accusations would not convince a judge, the various complainants were told. There was proof in almost all cases that the purchases and sales were made with the client's explicit consent. Those complainants got nowhere until two sisters who lived in Moose Factory, way up near James Bay, complained that many of the holdings (Pluman's Funeral Homes and Glacial Advances as just two examples) they had been sold were simply "not suitable" for retirement accounts of people in their late eighties as the sisters were.

Not suitable is a clumsy, vague, abstract term, true, but it is, in fact, one to be found in the glossary of the Ontario Securities Act. Then, and only then, did the regulators begin to pay heed. And, of course, so did many of those on The Street trained in litigation – investors were speaking their language, so to speak. Lawsuits streamed into the halls of justice in Old City Hall, just up the street. IED could barely keep enough red ink cartridges in stock for their dot-matrix printers.

One thorny issue kept raising its head. One of the first things Big Bobby did as CEO of IED was to take an idea of his twelve-year-old son's and have several thousand gold-and-blue stickers printed up.

@ IED U R #1

To shore up the IED brand, every account statement mailed out to clients had the sticker affixed to the first page. Several litigators jumped on the stickers as proof that this prestigious house had assumed a "fiduciary" duty. That is to say, the client's interest came before that of the company's.

That incensed Big Bobby. "Since when does advertising have anything to do with the facts let alone with any legal obligations? Advertising is just talk. Just words. How the hell could we flog our new issues or mutual funds offering us special commission with legal obligations like that hanging around our neck?"

Times continued to remain tough for the industry, and particularly for IED, for more than two and a half years. In a business where quarterly earnings reports seem separated by decades, two and a half years felt like a millennium.

"You wanna park your dough, Mr. McGregor?" asked Whacky Toulmin, a thirty-year veteran at IED, his head propped up by a phone receiver. "You'd like something safe and long-term? Okay, how about a one-hundred-and-eighty-day government treasury bill? Just keep your fingers crossed we both live long enough to see it mature."

In an attempt to shore up the cash-flow situation, the week before

Christmas 2002, CEO Big Bobby let go five of the reps' assistants, a procedure known around IED interchangeably as either "Awarding the Doric" or "Giving the Shaft."

That move didn't help things much. The bloated invoices of the lawyers hired to calm the regulatory agencies or defend the company in court more than offset any savings from staff reductions.

It didn't help either that revenues continued to shrink as client after client abandoned a vessel that had sailed so prestigiously since 1969. Those clients who didn't jump ship couldn't be made to buy or sell a share. The only thing they wanted was their money back. The only thing to increase at IED was the moaning of the reps as their prized "books of business" (the assets clients had invested through them) shrank. And that meant, of course, so did their commissions. Anyone who knows anything about investments knows stock markets go up and down. Yet reps/producers have great difficulty understanding why their paycheques should, too.

"Revenue's flatter than day-old Perrier on a plate" was the way Edgar Parsons, the vice-chairman, put it. Edgar had known good times and bad. He had begun his career in the investment business back in England, years before the founding of IED. Though well past manda-tory retirement, he became the vice-chairman when The Gentlemen of Panama left and took refuge in the sun-filled, pollution-free, tax-free climate of Central America.

"Negative growth" was what Head of Research Skly Cszymorska called it.

"Phrase it however you wish," Edgar retorted philosophically. "No company can survive on negative profits forever."

On the first Monday of June that year, a long-distance phone call came in. "Edgar, do us all a favour and dump Big Bobby. Today. Not tomorrow. Today. The job's too big for that dumb [redacted]. We should have realized that long ago. He has no idea how to run the company. To be honest, I'm not sure now that dumb [redacted] could run a red light. Kindly. Can you hear me? Kindly get somebody in there who can turn the [redacted] place around," counselled Chairman Sherwin Chable all the way from Panama City in a hoarse, typically menacing voice. You could almost see his jaw jutting defiantly forward.

"Or you know what?" Chairman Chable continued. "I'll come back up there and take charge of that shithouse again myself." He then pointed out that his "Mormon Knee" was acting up again and he was on his way out to an appointment with his kinesiologist. With no further encouragement or even a goodbye or cordial closing salutation of some kind, he hung up.

Say what you will about Vice-Chairman Parsons: he could take a hint. Not sixty seconds passed before Skly from his research office and the senior vice-president of sales, Don-Phil de Vita, jogged down the corridor and were buzzed into the executive suite. By mid-afternoon, the three-man Crisis Committee had hired a "search" consultant and was ready to find IED a new president. A brand-new president.

For the next few months, the committee met with the search consultant every Friday afternoon. After a second threat from the chairman to fly up and take over Big Bobby's office, the Crisis Committee, now called the Search Committee, reached agreement on two top-notch candidates, each with outstanding credentials. Each had a long list of accomplishment upon accomplishment in this brokerage firm or that bank. In essence, and for exactly the same reason, though using quite different language, both men refused to take on the CEO-ship of one of Canada's most prestigious investment dealers since 1969. They were, both explained, financial people, not miracle workers.

When word of the two refusals got out, Winnipeg emailed the Search Committee. It suggested that Toronto might be better off with an ad, stating the skill set required, in *SWAMI*, the trade journal of the Society for Wizards, Alchemists, Magicians, and Illusionists. And Winnipeg attached, thoughtfully enough, a hyperlink to the SWAMI website.

The budget-constrained, early-morning "au revoir" breakfast to award the glass Doric with a brass plate inscribed with Big Bobby's name in recognition of, as Edgar put it, "almost three decades" (twenty-three years to be exact) of outstanding dedication to IED Securities attracted a limited attendance. Hardly anyone showed up to see their CEO, Big Bobby, get "The Shaft." Many offered the same excuse: traffic was heavy that Monday morning. Come on now, everybody knows the traffic in any major city in the modern world always moves on Monday morning at half the speed of any other workday of the week.

Halvert Tulvin's "Goings-On" *World of Finance* column summed it up this way: "Few see IED's CEO EX-ed."

Late September 2003

Finally, after a long dinner, catered by Kayak, the three-star restaurant on the top floor of 370 Bay, two bottles of Dom Perignon, and a bottle of Pommard (Edgar's favourite), the three members of the Search/Crisis Committee came to an agreement a third time.

Edgar summed things up with, "Well, I must say he doesn't seem like a man who makes many concessions to prudence, but then that's the kind of person we need around here. I mean, if we hope to survive, we must learn to do things differently and that involves a certain amount of risk. It always does."

Shortly after nine o'clock that evening, a call went out. Zygmunt Adams happened to be in bed in his lovely new home, lovely new wife by his side.

Well, it wasn't really a new home, not in the sense that it was recently built. In fact, it was an old home built some eighty years before in a neighbourhood now back in fashion. And it was his house only in the sense that it was registered in his name. Considering the size of the line of credit secured by the house, it would be more accurate to say the bank owned it.

Also, the new wife in bed beside him was a new wife, no question, having married less than three months before. But she wasn't Zyg's wife, not in any sense of the word whatsoever. She had dropped in on her way home after an early-evening match at her tennis club.

Why, in such a situation, would Zygmunt answer the phone is beyond explanation except that it was such an odd time for someone to phone. Nine o'clock on a Friday? Not even the boldest telemarketer would call at that hour unless in search of one final rejection before calling it a night.

"Who in hell would phone on a Friday at this hour? Mind if I take it? Might be Harvey Markson from Bermuda. Been trying to get him all week."

Zyg let the phone ring a third time, then picked it up and said in a deep, modulated voice, "You have reached 968-7174, Zyg Adams's residence. If you would like to leave a message, please do so after the beep." Zyg made a beep sound.

"Oh, Zygmunt, good evening. It's Edgar Parsons down at IED Securities. We haven't spoken for some time. I wonder if you would be kind enough to give me a call at home this weekend. There's an important matter I'd like to discuss with you. Thanks. My number is –"

"Edgar, it's Zyg. How've you been? You're right. We haven't talked for some time."

"Zygmunt? Oh, Zygmunt, is that you? I thought I was getting your voice mail."

"I haven't gotten around to setting it up yet. Just wanted to make sure it wasn't a crank call. You never know these days."

"Yes, well, sorry to ring you so late. Frankly, I didn't expect you home on a Friday night."

"No problem, Edgar. I'm in for the evening."

Perhaps it was the Pommard. Edgar's voice boomed into the bedroom like that of a game-show announcer. Zyg held the phone away from his ear. Edgar cleared his throat.

"In confidence, Zygmunt, we've a bit of a challenge on our hands down here, you might or might not have heard. Big Bobby's a nice fellow, a wonderful bloke actually. But we've come to realize, however, the job's a bit much for him, you know. So he'll be leaving us shortly. What we need, we now realize, is strong all-round leadership, not just a hotshot of a salesman. We need a person who understands this business in all its aspects, not just sales. We all agree you have those qualifications and would make an excellent CEO. We think you'd be someone who could move our little company forward."

3
Zygmunt? Zygmunt Who?

Some eighteen years before in the early spring of 1985, from Freblis, a tiny hamlet thirty miles northeast of Frankfurt, Germany, upon the citizenry of Toronto was thrust Zygmunt Artur Adambrowski, a love affair back home gone sour.

At the age of twenty-three Herr Adambrowski abandoned his studies in the last year to become a *Wirtshraftsprüfer*, an accountant, and took his oversized dreams and his scarred heart somewhere else in search of what he was not quite sure. He knew one thing: the only known cure for scarred hearts was time. And when the young *Wirtshraftsprüfer* calculated how long it would take to heal his heart – he was good with numbers – it worked out to be, plus or minus a couple of years, an eternity.

So instead of time, he thought to try time's fellow-traveller, space, as a cure-all. His father had died several years earlier and his mother remarried and moved to Hamburg. A spinster aunt completely immersed in her medical practice was the only relative left in Freblis. There was nothing to hold him there.

Only the mangling of common idioms such as "from the kettle into the fire." Or "noisy" rather than "Nosey" Parker. Or "freezing your knickers off," rather than the more correct "knackers off." Or reference one day at lunch to a couple of women in the cafeteria as "hot potatoes," rather than the more correct "hot tomatoes," betrayed that English wasn't his native tongue. He arrived in Canada with not a trace of an accent, little money, but with a highly developed appreciation of speed – fast cars, fast horses, and fast potatoes.

Should fame arrive one day, as he expected it would, how much easier to sign autographs with an abbreviated Adambrowski, he reasoned, whereas it was highly unlikely, wherever he ended up, there would be another Zygmunt. (IED's former CEO, president, and chief equity strategist, Big Bobby Little, showed how far out of touch he was with the industry: when told of his replacement, he asked in his bewilderment, "Zygmunt? Zygmunt who?") At this point, though, Zyg Adams's only significant possession was his name.

When he arrived in Canada, Zyg knew he wouldn't be starting at the top. Good thing, too. It was his love of horses and an ad in the *Daily Racing Form* that landed him his first job: assistant head dishwasher at the Woodbine Racetrack. For grooms, hot walkers, other stable hands, outriders, groundskeepers, jockeys, trainers, breeders, owners, hangers-on (mostly media people), and various track officials, Zyg plied his new profession in the cafeteria next to the backstretch. He always showed up for work at least fifteen minutes early and always worked past quitting time. And he always left his workplace spotless. On his day off, if asked by the head dishwasher to help out, without a second's thought Zyg would agree.

On his early-morning breaks from the clanking, sweaty, sour-smelling, vapour-filled business of un-soiling dishes, he'd slip over to a spot on the backstretch rail to watch the horses work out. The smell of damp earth and mown grass always excited him. As horses clomped by, urged on by the shrill cries and whistles of their riders, Zygmunt would clock their speed with an old-fashioned silver stopwatch given to him by his maternal grandfather, a well-known veterinarian back in Germany. The information gleaned from that watch – especially when it differed from that of the track's official clocker – led to many a conversation and many a new acquaintance. Some of them took him for a jockey who couldn't "make weight." Most of them were decent people devoted to horses and the sport of horse racing; some of them, though, like some of the horses, were somewhat fast.

One new acquaintance was Clifford Lloyd Sutton, a stooped-over, plump-faced man in his late fifties. Antacid pills taken to balance his daily overload of Seagram's Crown Royal rye produced small white bubbles parked regularly in the corners of his mouth. Mr. Cliffy had made a sizable fortune from the promotion and sale of shares of several small gold mines, Silver Lake Gold being the best known and for him the most successful.

Despite the promising hints of early assays of 3.7 grams of ore per tonne, the company's haphazard exploration program failed to unearth another trace with a core anywhere near that degree of concentration. The treasury bare by the spring of 1987, the mining company failed to submit financial statements, mandatory under Regulation 523(b)ii, section 109a, item iii(c). Three and a half months later the Vancouver Stock Exchange delisted the company's shares. *DIG*, the Bible of the mining industry, lambasted Silver Lake for its slipshod corporate practices, which under any other regulatory regime outside of Zimbabwe's would have prompted an investigation for mismanagement, if not outright fraud, and claimed that shareholders who held on to their shares lost their "life savings."

"Ever hear such bullcrap," Mr. Cliffy was overheard to have retorted with his Crown Royal raspiness, his indignation at a full gallop. "I should sue the buggers. Nobody ever heard of diversification? Would folks come out here to the track and bet their whole bundle on one horse in the first race? Of course not. Nobody's that stupid. Nobody lost their life savings. That's just typical newspaper bullcrap, that's all." After he uttered such quips, a smile of insightfulness would light up his face, revealing an unexpected large gap between his front teeth.

Mr. Cliffy himself had diversified very well. Acquisition fees and a handsome executive salary diverted enough of Silver Lake's capital into his hands so that he was able to hold on to his hobbled brokerage firm. And when the plug was finally pulled on old Silver Lake, he had no trouble holding on to his breeding farm, Noblesse Oblige, and his stable of eleven horses – five geldings, five broodmares, and a twelve-year-old stallion named Lucky Hot (by Seven Sevens out of Firepot Phyllis).

The racing reputation of Noblesse Oblige Farms rested upon neither great lineage nor great speed. The ownership of most of the inhabitants had been "claimed" away from other stables by Mr. Cliffy and most often out of the last race of the day. Of course, by that time in the afternoon, Mr. Cliffy's judgment of horseflesh was usually way, way off course. One exception, Booze and Snooze, a nifty, little, late-born brown colt, friskier than a narco cop, looked in his morning workouts as if he could run faster than the wind. Unfortunately, in his first big race, the Appleton Stakes, a two-furlong dash, poor Booze and Snooze, about to take the lead at the top of the homestretch, lost his footing on the "cuppy" turf and fell, his left hind leg broken. The track veterinarian put him down on the spot. However the backstretch folk felt about Mr. Cliffy – he had his supporters – they admitted a change of luck was due him.

"A guy like you, Zyg, who gets along with people, people who like to take a little risk now and again, could double his paycheque in no time flat down at my company," Mr. Cliffy said a week later matter-of-factly, staring straight ahead, his leather-padded elbows resting on the backstretch rail. "People need someone to help them realize their dreams. Comfortable retirements, fancy cottages, homes in Florida, world travel, golf club memberships, large inheritances for the children. Whatever. Or, if they already have enough, then we try to make them richer than in their wildest dreams. That's what we do mostly."

Mr. Cliffy dabbed the sides of his mouth with a handkerchief. "Help make people's dreams come true. That can be a truly excellent way to earn a living. Once you learned the ropes, you'd be good, damn good. Double, maybe triple, your pay in six months, a year at the most."

The sweep hand of his grandfather's stopwatch didn't have to jerk forward twice before Zyg agreed to the idea. Assistant head dishwashers at a racetrack don't make much money. Even a quadrupled salary would have been a step up – not an enormous one in the scheme of things, but a start.

That turned out to be Clifford Sutton's lucky day in another way. That afternoon Mr. Cliffy's horses won two races and made enough to feed the members of Noblesse Oblige for the rest of the year. It was a Saturday.

Mr. Cliffy wanted Zyg to begin work at his company the following

Monday. Zyg refused to leave his cafeteria job before a replacement assistant head dishwasher was found. It was almost a month before he joined Sutton Securities as the administrative assistant to Chicky Glickerman. That would be the second and the last time Zyg would ever be an assistant to anybody. But the pilgrimage from Germany to make his own dreams come true had begun a steep upward climb.

Zyg was off and running.

■ ■ ■

Up until the mid-1980s, the top salesmen at Sutton Securities were called "big dogs." The branding expert Mr. Cliffy brought in felt that name no longer apt. The two men came up with plaques that read:

MEMBER
SUTTON SECURITIES' CIRCLE
Constantly Committed
to the
Care of
and
Concern for
the
Client

On the plastic fob of the gold key ring presented to all members called into "The Circle," the traditional picture of Goofy was replaced by a furry St. Bernard with five little c's inside a circle burned into the staves of the wooden cask under its chin. The qualifications for admission remained at gross commissions of $800,000 earned in the previous calendar year.

Only the name of the group and the key fob changed. Nothing else.

That Chicky Glickerman could be a member of the 5-C Circle – a Five C'er – was a good thing. The five-bedroom house in Moore Park (one of

Toronto's "more prestigious neighbourhoods," proclaimed the ad for the house four doors down, which sold for $108,000 over asking); an Aston Martin and a Ford utility vehicle; the Tyrolean ski chalet on twenty-two acres on the outskirts of Creemore, almost eighty miles north of the city; *The Carenought*, a twenty-nine-foot yacht moored at the Cherry Beach Yacht Club (known as "The Dump" in memory of its former land use); eight-year-old twin daughters from his marriage to an Australian girl, and from a prior marriage, two boys (one with a serious speech impediment), both in college; his membership in the highly selective Provincial Club; the odd charitable donation for marketing reasons; and all those expenses plus the everyday ones of a household that included a housekeeper and various service people to keep the garden lush and the pool clean, plus an active social life since his wife liked to *pah-tee* (not all the entertainment expenses tax-deductible) required – better, necessitated – enough in gross commissions for Chicky to be a Five C'er as a minimum, as an absolute bare minimum.

After his first wife moved back home to Newfoundland, a sunny-dispositioned girl from Canberra in her mid-twenties on a slow trip around the world took up residence in the basement of Chicky's home as the children's nanny.

Two weeks later the nanny moved up a step, more precisely, two whole flights of stairs. She and her long blond hair and her cocoa tan began to share the king-size bed of the master bedroom. Not long after that, a marriage took place, and not long after that, two very blond non-identical baby girls also took up residence in the Glickerman household.

Chicky had connections: private schoolmates such as Cross Bennett (who introduced Chicky to Mr. Cliffy), fraternity brothers from Pi Iota Theta ("The Pits"), and from the sports clubs he joined over the years. Still, that he, "Slicky," as the Back Office referred to him, had enough "production" to become a member of the chairman's 5-C Circle rested on a fluke.

His many connections helped little, especially after he lost money for most of his friends in his early days learning the investment business. What got him into the 5-C Circle was his discovery of a marketing niche: charity. Not his own, of course, other people's.

A woman he dated in the days between his two marriages induced – perhaps seduced – him into sitting on the board of the Mental Hygiene Association. When the incumbent chairman of finance moved to the West Coast, the office fell to Chicky as the only director with a financial background of any sort.

He had taken two years of commerce and finance before joining his father's importing business (an endeavour he found as boring as the accounting courses he failed at university). But give Chicky credit. He was the first board member to take the trouble to question the executive director's expense account. On a tip, he had a special audit performed. It turned out that while most of the association's volunteers were extremely conscientious and hard-working fundraisers, the voluntary efforts of one particular volunteer, after elaborate dinners at the association's expense, were put forth mostly in the bed of the executive director and raised something other than funds. The executive director resigned shortly after that and went on to become a consultant in the executive search business.

Half a million dollars in Government of Canada bonds with maturity eighteen years away purchased just before a quick drop in interest rates (one of his two recommendations for Mental Hygiene's building fund) showed a nice profit and to no one's surprise more than Chicky's. His other recommendation, a block of stock in Federal Wealth and Great Trust dropped a little in price almost immediately, but within a month showed an impressive gain. Of course, Chicky did not act as the broker on those transactions. That would have presented a conflict of interest.

Something much better than simple commissions came out of it all, though. With those two solid recommendations plus the discovery of the executive director's overburdened expense account, a pattern of Chicky's financial astuteness branded itself in the minds of several other people involved in charity work.

The first one to acknowledge Chicky's talent was the association's chairman, whose family investments had suffered greatly under the stewardship of the Great Trust Company of Canada, which went into bankruptcy and was forced to merge with Federal Wealth. He asked

Chicky to take over management of a little more than half of his family's assets.

Chicky's reputation grew along with the upward trend in stock prices. "He's done very nicely by my family," the association's chairman might say, and to more than one business associate. Not long after that, Chicky was recommended as one of several financial advisers for the Metropolitan Hospital's endowment fund. Recommendations followed from the Good Citizens' Club, the Museum of Modern Fashion, and the Metropolitan Museum of Art, though he would have never heard of, say, Paul Cézanne, Jackson Pollock, or even the renowned Toronto sculptor and muralist Sengli Timovitz. Not only did those charities become clients, so did members of their finance committees and other volunteers. A quiet assuredness emanated from Chicky's voice when he spoke about the capital markets. Most often he would deploy a quote from Sutton's two-man research department: "We believe over the next two to five years the market will climb to … There'll be ups and downs along the way, of course."

The only problem with all that marketing strategy was almost every other week Chicky had to attend charity dinners and galas where the chairman of the convenors' committee thanked every last person who had lifted a finger for the event. Chicky never ducked out, though, without at least one new business contact. He had his "marketing" rules:

- Always open conversation with a compliment usually about dress.
- Have prepared a non-financial topic or two (not the weather).
- Always carry a drink in the left hand to avoid a soggy handshake.
- Always carry an adequate supply of biz cards.
- Sell charm, not stocks.
- Never leave an event without at least one contact to follow up on.

Often he carried his drink in the wrong hand. The one new contact, though, was an ironclad rule.

He knew he had uncovered an ocean of potential clients in the world of charities. To keep his own little pond from drying up, he knew he needed a constant trickle of prospects. This was not the kind of fortune-amassing greed critics so typically – and facilely – ascribe to Bay Street brokers and dealmakers and the like. Chicky's "production" allowed him to survive. This wasn't a case of greed. No, it was one of need. Whatever else could he do? Cut down on the *pah-tee-ing*?

"Chicky, I love all the commissions you bring in, don't get me wrong," said Mr. Cliffy one morning. "But you know what? You're going to burn yourself out. You need an assistant."

"Nope. Cost too much if I have to share commissions."

"A full-time assistant would free you up for more marketing with your charity friends. The whole idea would be you'd make more money with a lot less effort. Just try it for a few months."

"Maybe, maybe. All that new compliance crap drives me nuts. But if it's going to cost me money, forget it. And whoever it is, has got to be bright. I don't want to spend half my time trying to train some ninny," said Chicky in a whiny grunt that slipped out over a lower lip that drooped permanently.

"I have just the man for you. He's somebody people like instantly. And he's bright. Bright as a summer's day."

1986

"Who's calling?"

"Sir, it's Zygmunt Adams, sir. Sutton Securities, sir. Hope I'm not disturbing you, sir. Just following up on the invitation we sent you a few days ago. For an evening with Chicky Glickerman a week Thursday? Dinner at the King Eddy? Mr. Glickerman has some proven ideas on how to make money in the challenging markets we're facing right now. Cocktails at seven. Then dinner. No obligation on your part, sir. No obligation whatsoever." Zyg paused. "Would you be interested, sir, in any way?"

"Yes, I would be. Very much so. And you know why?" There was a short pause but not long enough to wedge in a response. "Because I want to come down there and break somebody's neck."

"Why … why would you want to do that, sir?" Zyg asked without flinching. "You sound like a reasonable man."

"Part of my marketing strategy," the man replied matter-of-factly. "I'm an orthopedic surgeon." Then, in a muffled shout, his words clipped: "Look, I'll come down there and break yours, too, if you guys don't stop calling me. I've asked you a dozen-dozen times. 'Do not call me. Do. Not. Call. Me. Ever-ever again.' I have no interest in Sutton Securities. None. None whatsoever. Somebody else looks after my investments. The last thing on this earth I need is dinner with your Dicky Cumbersome."

"Chicky Glickerman, sir. And, as a doctor, sir, you certainly know the value of a second opinion at times. I'll have your name removed from our list, sir," Zyg said, trying to knead the objections like pie dough. "But Mr. Glickerman is very knowledgeable and has years of experience –"

The phone line crackled with repeated attempts to slam the receiver into its cradle, while in the background could be heard: "Will those stupid bastards ever leave me alone?"

People die. Or worse. In Chicky's opinion, some client's nephew gets into the business and steals his aunt's account from you. Or after the market turns sour for a few months, some aggressive know-nothing, in Chicky's opinion, from some other brokerage house entices a client away with assurances of earning back the packet lost under your mentorship. Or people move away. One reason reps/producers like Chicky remain in The Circle as Five C'ers is they recognize the ongoing need for a steady supply of replacement clients.

From the day it first opened its doors, Sutton Securities once a month took the entire second page of *The Community Crier*, a giveaway newspaper delivered to homes in the three wealthiest neighbourhoods of the city. Above a picture of a happy grey-haired couple seated in front of a blazing home fire, their gaze fixed on the half-dozen travel brochures in their hands, a question in thirty-point type was posed: "Will it be Hawaii or the Himalayas?" (which Chicky pronounced as the *HIM-all-yuhs*). Below the joyous couple, the copy read: "Sound investing will get you there. Safely. Every time."

In smaller print appeared a coupon offer for an audiocassette entitled *Sound Investing: The Ten Principles*. The wording never changed. Nor did the picture of the fireplace, nor of the contented couple by then probably well into their late nineties and in some nursing home on the island of Oahu or in downtown Kathmandu.

Interested dreamers need only send in the ad's coupon and shortly *The Ten Principles* would arrive by first-class mail ("strike while the iron is hot," Mr. Cliffy insisted in spite of the expense). Two or three business days later the respondent would get a call. If that person for some reason turned down the opportunity to discuss his or her dreams as well as his or her current investment holdings (in the comfort of home or Sutton's offices), the respondent's name went on the "sweetheart" list. Once on that list, the respondent would be contacted every year, sometimes twice a year, by one or other of Sutton's reps. The only reliable way to get your name off that list was to move away, far away, or die. Death was by far the more successful strategy, since as long as you resided within an hour's drive of the city, a Sutton rep, with the efficiency of a top-notch investigative reporter, would track you and your unfulfilled dreams down.

Sutton's primary form of attack was the face-to-face meeting. If that couldn't be arranged, then the next line was special seminars – with or without dinner thrown in – to foster direct contact with the prospective client. Even in a short pre-seminar chat, one could find out if the client had ambitions of buying a country house in the Dordogne, retiring at forty, leaving all twelve children independently wealthy, ascending Mount Everest, or providing for a life expectancy of a hundred and twenty. Given the need, it was just a matter of demonstrating that someone as skilled as Chicky could come up with the "investment strategies and ideas" that would carry one's savings toward that life goal no matter how far-fetched.

"No such thing as too many clients," Chicky claimed. "You can always winnow." So, despite the commissions his charity work generated, he hoped Zygmunt, among other duties, would uncover a few "High Net Worths" – individuals with a million dollars or more to invest, the species of *Homo sapiens* that makes a big producer's time productive.

Around the dinner hour, Mondays and Wednesdays, Zygmunt would call people on the sweetheart list. To warm up, he'd call the most hopeless ones first, people who hadn't taken the trouble to fill in their phone numbers on the cut-out coupon from *The Community Crier* ad. In an evening, he might make five or six dozen calls to those who, at one time or other in their lives, had requested *The Ten Principles*.

"Free food and drink? And all I have to do is listen to you guys yak on about investments. Sounds delightful. What's your name again, son?"

"Zygmunt. Zygmunt Adams, sir."

"Well, look, I'm a little busy this month, Zygmunt. Mind if I skip your seminar this time round?"

"You'd be interested some other time?"

"Yes, of course. Why don't you call me back?"

"When would you suggest, sir?"

"How about early January 2050?"

Zyg tapped out another phone number. *Click-click-click-click.* Then another. And another. Eleven in all before he made contact with something other than an answering machine.

"How nice of you. May I ask what time does it begin, dear?" a sweet-toned voice asked."

"Drinks at seven for dinner at eight," Zyg replied.

"Oh, my goodness, that's a little late. I'm eighty-six. I never go out after dark. If you have an afternoon tea one day, dear, I'd love to."

Click-click-click-click.

"You lot? I lost a ruddy fortune in '74 with the likes of you. Nothing but a bunch of flaming thugs, you lot."

Click-click-click.

Some nights even the wildest of dreamers had no need of Chicky Glickerman's financial perspicacity. That didn't seem to bother Zyg. He had become inured to the turndowns. It was a numbers game: just keep dialling, and sooner or later, an interested party would show up. And don't be in any hurry to take no for an answer. It was all part of the training – getting used to rejection. Who was it that said nothing equips you better for this world than a thousand rejections? Maybe it was Chicky.

Tuesdays and Thursdays Zyg would leave early to catch the subway up to his M.B.A. class at the university. That left the weekends during that first year for M.B.A. assignments, meetings with classmates on projects, and still finding time somehow to do the assignments for his securities licence.

Two of the Goslings, as the regulars of the Wild Goose Tavern called themselves, about four blocks from the racetrack, complained: "We never see you around here anymore, Zyg. You fallen in love or something?"

Before Sutton, when still working at the cafeteria, Zyg was a Gosling himself, a regular who showed up three or four nights a week. With his current workload, however, he only came in occasionally and only late on a Saturday night at that, and not so much to chat as in search of an overnight companion, though with greater success than he had cold-calling. Around the Wild Goose you could quickly get an idea who'd be interested in your services and who wouldn't.

By late spring the following year, Zyg had obtained his securities license (91 percent average) and completed the first year of his M.B.A. (82 percent), much of the content he had covered before in his *Wirtshraftsprüfer* studies back in Germany. Though he had received not one word of encouragement from Chicky from the first day on, Zyg began to feel good about his new profession.

He'd caught on to the cold-call business. And he felt at home in the Sutton Securities' crisis-of-the-moment atmosphere – stocks plunging, stocks soaring, opportunities taken, opportunities missed, things delivered on time or not on time – a stew of good and bad events from early morning until the end of day. Rain or shine, something always going on – an office lottery or a two-hundred-point drop in the market, a hot "initial public offering" or an unfavourable earnings report. Boredom never showed its face around Sutton. Not for a second.

And Zyg didn't mind all the chores Chicky assigned him: taking messages all day, hunting down share certificates or cheques that went astray, trade confirmations or tax slips that got lost, letters, research reports, prospectuses and memos that needed to be sent out. Sometimes Chicky needed tickets for a hockey game or basketball or baseball, at others times reservations for lunch or dinner or a court time.

That was all part of what it was to be an assistant to Charles "Chicky" Glickerman, Sutton's second-highest "producer" and a proud member of Sutton Securities' Circle of Constantly Committed to the Care of and Concern for the Client – that ruddy, flaming lot.

For Zyg, The Street was starting to feel like a home.

1987

Around 4:30 one Friday, after a phone chat with one of the new clients Zyg had brought in, Chicky, his lower lip drooping more than usual, decided to have a word with his assistant.

"This isn't working. Simply t'aint working. All the goddamn people you've brought in want nothing but savings accounts on steroids. I'm not a bank teller. I need people who want to make real money, for Chrissake. I can't make any dough selling government bonds. If they don't want any risk, they're the wrong people for me. They need a psychiatrist, not a broker. I have bills to pay. Lots, believe me."

Chicky shuffled sheets of paper in and out of his attaché case. Not once during the conversation did Chicky look up except to peruse the legs of a secretary who walked by his office. "You can have all the new clients you brought in. And Mr. Cliffy has agreed to pay you a salary for the next few months while you build a clientele."

"How do I do that? I don't have the connections you have."

"Do what I did. Join a few charities."

"I don't know anybody in a charity."

"Well, get to know the people at your church."

"I don't go to church."

Chicky fingered the gold chain around his neck until he found something to fix his gaze on – his watch. "Jesus, I'm on court in thirty minutes," he said, his sleepy eyes coming to life. He threw his morning newspaper, opened at the comics, into his attaché case, slammed the lid shut, and fastened it.

"Find a hobby. Polo. Or vintage cars. Something with people who have real dough," he said, then dashed off to catch the elevator as if it was the last chance out before the Gestapo came in and arrested everyone with a slack lower lip.

■ ■ ■

On a chilly fall day, two months later, at "The Temple for Too Slow Horses," as Lance Warburton called Woodbine Racetrack, right after the fourth race when the hopes of most of the attendees customarily began to fade, Zyg climbed the stairs to row 12 of section H in the General Admission stand.

That was the area where the truck drivers, bartenders, waiters, maintenance men, barbers, deliverymen, couriers, construction workers, electricians, and cabbies, the true fans of horse racing, gathered. Unlike the people above in the Members' Section or the Directors' Lounge, those in General Admission made bets that, if not successful, could make a difference – a significant difference – to their daily lives. The unsuccessful bets of the people – players – upstairs wouldn't alter their dinner plans one bit. But bettors in General Admission put their souls on the line. If their judgment was off and, for example, the shopping money disappeared, that could turn a slow day for the coroner very busy.

On the other hand, a winning bet pumped into your very being a feeling of omnipotence. When the horse on which you placed your hard-come-by money slipped across the finish line first by, say, a head (and no inquiry sign flashed up on the tote board to put the victory in question), it seemed as if you and all nature had merged in a moment of joy, a moment in which all adversity lay vanquished in a moment of pure, unsullied contentment.

"Zyg! For Chrissake, I thought you'd left town or croaked. Where you been, for Chrissake? Oh, I know. The one place I forgot to look. Down on Bay Street, down with all the big shots. Too busy for your old buddies with boots covered in horseshit."

Lance's six-foot-four frame loomed over Zyg as he slid into the row. Lance slapped Zyg on the back. "Backstretch's not the same without you, old buddy. Nobody to goddamn tell us who's got a little extra lick in their stride and who hasn't. Nice to see you, though. Hey, how come you didn't bring that good looker with you? She smarten up and ditch you?"

34

"Why would you say that?" Zyg asked as he sat down.

"You look so glum. That's not you."

"Whacked out, that's all. My new job doesn't leave much time for sleep let alone women."

"You certainly don't look like the same guy who chased those two sisters from the Warsaw riding team all around the Royal Winter Fair last year. Remember? I got nowhere. But you earned the 'Pole Vaulter of the Month' Award."

"I don't have time for women these days."

"No time for women? That must be one helluva an important job you got. What are you now? The president of Canada or something? A guy like you, who hammered just about every female around here who wasn't nailed down, doesn't give women up unless something very, very important comes along." The grey ponytail, held together by a black elastic band, bounced up and down on Lance's back.

"The guy I work for, worked for, wants – wanted – ten hours a day from me," Zyg explained. "On top of that, I've got hours and hours of studying to do, so I hadn't talked to her in months. When I called, she was quite hostile."

"You know better than to neglect women," Lance said. "Too bad. She was cute. What a shame. Maybe I should give her a call. She might prefer someone good-looking and who has a thorough understanding of horses – and women."

Whether using the word *love* rightly or not, people who knew Lance Warburton would say he loved animals. Of *Homo sapiens*, he preferred friends and females. Of all other species on earth, he preferred horses by far.

As the manager of Crawshort Stables, he spent all his days attending to the needs of the horses in his care. At night he read about horses, anything in print from *American Bloodstock* to *Tackroom Tactics*. If asked, he would volunteer quite readily that nobody in Canada knew more about the care and breeding of Thoroughbreds. He was always on the lookout for contaminated water, harmful plants, and small hard-to-detect leg wounds. He kept his stables immaculate, and he never hesitated for a moment to pick up a shovel and muck out a stall, leaving only the bedding. What he removed he called "Danish topsoil," an expression meant to get the goat of his friend from Denmark, Billy Mayer, known better as "His Worship."

The traditional *dutta-dutta-dutta-dahhhh* bleated through the stands. A string of horses filed out onto the dirt track and out from the shadow of the stands that fell halfway across. The jockeys wore shirts and caps of bright red, chartreuse, yellow, yellow and chartreuse, dark green, white, white and black – colours framed in all kinds of geometric shapes, polka dots, stripes, bands, crosses, and outsized letters of the alphabet. Except for one smaller horse that kept twisting and turning, the entrants for the fifth race sauntered past the stands in a line. The crowd began to murmur.

"Jesus, Jesus. Jesus. I hope I break even today, Zyg. I'm not kidding. If I lose serious dough today, I'll have to give up women or the ponies. I can't lose. That's all there is to it. Life would be shitty without women."

"Your wife probably wouldn't mind," said Zyg, not looking up from his program.

Since the beginning of time, some regulars said, a threesome of men had gathered in the first three seats in row 12 in Section H of the General Admission stand of Woodbine every Sunday afternoon of the racing season. Acquaintances would wander over to say hello or to get an opinion on who might be the winner of the next race. An earlier member of the triumvirate had dropped out and gone to work in the Alberta oil fields. Lance had brought Zyg in as the replacement.

"Where's His Worship?" Zyg asked. "He told me he'd be here. Said he wanted to talk to me about something."

"Something must have come up," Lance replied.

"That's not like him. He's always on time."

"If His Worship says he'll be here, he'll be here." Lance drew a large *X* across the history of a horse in his copy of the day's *Racing Form*. "More dogs on the card today than at the Humane Society. Next thing you know, they'll have an electric bunny out there for them to chase. I mean, who's to like here?"

"Take a look at the seven horse."

"Dawn of Creation?" Just crossed her out. *Woof-woof.* Dawny's a dog. Hates the distance. Hates it. Take a look at the four horse. Look at the breeding. Great genes. One small problem, she can't go the distance, either. You gotta like those genes, though. Her grandpa set a track record here for the six furlongs. Look at those genes. Probably descended from the Darley Arabian. I mean, wow!"

"Genes, genes. That all you ever think about," said a pudgy man with a freckled face and a well-kempt blond pompadour who took the aisle seat next to Lance.

"Be kind to him, Your Worship," Zyg said as they shook hands. "The poor guy's probably going to have to give up women today."

"Give up women? Lance? Not while he's still breathing."

"Did you bet?" Lance asked Your Worship.

"Yup. The three."

"*Woof-woof*. The three's a dog, Your Worship," Lance said. "I've told you a hundred times. Always talk to me before you bet. The three'll be glue before the summer's out. Glue, for sure."

"You know what I can't figure out, Lance?" His Worship said. "Why a fine handicapper like yourself hasn't made you and the rest of us so bloody wealthy it'd be a miracle one of those Bay Street sharpies hadn't found us."

His Worship was considerably older than Lance. He was stocky, five-nine or so, a little taller than Zyg, with a concentration of weight around the hips. When he smiled, as he often did, his mouth revealed brownish teeth that camouflaged a natural intelligence behind them. He'd been a trainer – an outstanding one – before he got involved with the Horsemen's Protective Society and ended up as its president. If you ever needed advice or needed someone to plead your cause, Billy Mayer, His Worship, was the first person around the track you'd turn to.

"They're at the post," a loud, deep-toned voice announced over the public-address system. The crowd's murmur grew. "They're off!"

Ten minutes later in the bar His Worship shook his head. "That kid on my horse took her wide on the clubhouse turn. Too inexperienced. I know better than to bet on bug riders."

The heavy smell of fresh and recycled alcohol fumes filled the room, the chatter too loud to identify the music in the background. "Zyg, before our equine encyclopedia comes over, I called yesterday because I gotta talk to you. Our goddamn pension fund over at the society is in a holy mess. A complete goddamn mess, let me tell you. When the members find out, they'll go bananas. Some Bay Street jerk, a friend of some guy's brother-in-law, screwed us blind. He's got us holding all kinds of shit. 'Don't worry, don't worry,' he kept telling us.

"But last month we got hammered. Really hammered. When the bottom dropped out of the market, our goddamn pension fund fell through the floor. We've got to do something. Yeah, we know you're green in the business. We know all that. But at least we know we can goddamn trust you." His Worship leaned back. "You're one of us, not some fancy financial jerkwater with payments due on his fancy-dancy BMW. But, Zyg, Jesus boy, don't breathe a word of this. Shit, here comes Lance. I'm out of town tomorrow. Call me Tuesday first thing, will you? See what you think you can do for us."

"*Woof-woof*, dog lovers," said Lance, a sheaf of $20 bills fanned out in his hand. "Would you give me the pleasure of purchasing a nice cold libation for the two of you who never could tell the difference between a winning horse and a pile of Danish topsoil. Losing can work up quite a thirst, I'm told."

"Lance, you always bet favourites. I like decent odds," said Zyg, announcing a bias that didn't allow him to cash a ticket the rest of the day. Of his other bets, one, for example, lost by a nose, another stumbled coming out of the starting gate and finished fifth. Still, the brief conversation with His Worship made Zyg feel he'd cashed winning tickets in all five of the last races.

■ ■ ■

"Unions got dough coming out their ying-yangs," said Mr. Cliffy on Monday, then dabbed his mouth with a fresh handkerchief and took another antacid pill. "You get yourself in good with one of those and you, my friend, will have struck pay dirt. You will have struck the motherlode." Mr. Cliffy paused for a moment and then said with a straight face, "You know what, Zyg? You might be the first person in history who ever struck a union?"

"They need help. Badly. Really badly."

"Of course, they do. When the market falls apart like this, that's what they all say. All they want is their money back, that's all. Same old story. Heard it a hundred times. My advice to them? Don't play with matches if you can't stand a little heat now and again."

"What do I do? Put them in some mutual funds or something?"

"No, I think I've got just the guy to help you – provided he likes you."

"Provided he likes me?"

"This guy knows more about stock markets than 99 percent of the bozos on The Street. Or any mucky-muck chief investment officer. He's obsessed with markets, anything to do with chance. But he's not quite so fond of people." Mr. Cliffy laughed again. "He's obsessed with markets. He's got this rocket scientist's brain along with enough allergies to make you think he should be on a life-support program."

■ ■ ■

Herself an only child, Emily Kopsin Shurtz gave birth later in life to her only child and to that child she gave her maiden name. In her mind, Kopsin Theodore Shurtz arrived on this earth with only one great mission on his small shoulders: to carry on the work of Kopsin and Kopsin LLP, her family's generation-old law practice. When he graduated from law school, gold medal in hand, a bright future seemed straight ahead of him. But he lacked enthusiasm for the problems that arise when family members try to take advantage of one another and start fighting. He abandoned the old family firm even though his uncles agreed to rename the firm Kopsin, Kopsin & Kopsin T. Shurtz LLP.

Federal Wealth (not yet merged with the Great Trust of Canada), the second-largest investment dealer in the country, owned by one of the five large banks, had always wanted somebody with brains in its organization. Once Federal Wealth learned of Kopsin's gold medal, it scooped him up like the last jujube in the candy dish on the receptionist's desk. The firm placed him in what came to be called the Investment Banking Division but at the time was known as the Underwriting Department. His mother could never quite figure out what business her son was in. She told her friends he'd found work in a funeral home.

For Kopsin, unfortunately though, the work seemed no different from the practice of law except, he claimed, with Federal's underwritings, you knew in advance who was going to get the short end of the stick. He stayed at Federal for three and a half years until one day he read Sutton's ad in *The World of Finance*'s classified section of the need for a compliance officer, corporate secretary, and equity strategist – all rolled into one preferably. With his legal training and investment banking background, Kopsin was the most logical candidate, in Cliffy Sutton's eyes, if only for his extremely modest salary demands.

The fact that Kopsin would get to spend most of his day with numbers suited him just fine. For him, numbers, when converted to charts, became things of beauty, revelations of how the world, at least the financial world, worked. He could find meaning in what looked to the untrained eye like the electrocardiogram of someone at death's door. The part about being a lawyer he never liked was gambling with other people's lives. But helping people gamble with their savings was an entirely different kind of undertaking, one that his mother still thought not much different from working in a funeral parlour.

Mr. Cliffy had recognized Kopsin's talent immediately. Within six months the house's portion of the commissions generated by his weekly bulletin of trading ideas more than offset the entire cost of the compliance officer/corporate secretary/equity strategist. Since Kopsin could barely manage himself, however, Mr. Cliffy never gave a thought to having him manage anyone else. What Kopsin could manage were investment portfolios, and he did that brilliantly. With that activity, however, a small problem existed in those days. If one of Sutton's "institutional" clients, say, a trust company or an insurance firm, suspected Sutton employed someone to manage portfolios for clients, Sutton would have been considered a competitor. Insurance and trust companies would never award a competitor trades that generated commissions. Kopsin had to practise his craft in the shadows.

Zyg knocked on the glass panel beside the door of Kopsin's office, and Kopsin waved him in.

"I'm on the phone with Rabbi Blunther," said Kopsin, his hand over the receiver. Then he coughed in sputters. "Just left me a message.

Whenever he thinks he's delivered a powerful sermon, he calls me to go short the pork bellies."

Kopsin coughed some more, then took his hand away from the receiver. "Oh, hi, Rabbi, it's Kopsin. Kopsin T. Shurtz from Sutton Securities." (The *T* was inserted to avoid confusion with some other Kopsin Shurtz calling from Sutton Securities.) "Rabbi, you called me ..."

The sides of the three large, heavily scratched grey filing cabinets, the sides of two tall teak bookcases and the worn desk, and the glass panel beside the door provided the only vertical planes in the office that didn't have charts taped, pinned, or clamped onto them. Almost anything that fluctuated numerically was represented by graphs or charts of one type or another, two of which – stock prices in New York and gold prices in London – went back to the early 1800s. The office of Kopsin T. Shurtz was turned into a shrine to the sacredness of data, with charts of oil and gold prices; charts of stock market indices (the Dow Jones, the Nikkei from Japan, the FTSE from London); charts that showed inflation, interest, and exchange rates; charts displaying "price-to-earnings" ratios since 1926; line charts, large and small, some in red, some in green, some in red and green, some in yellow and dark blue and black, others in plain black, like cave etchings of an ancient sect.

In the bookcases, the Bible of technical analysis and charts, written by Edwards and McGee (1948 edition), and the Bible of fundamental analysis by Graham and Dodd (1962 edition), sat upright, their spines vertical. Many other books lay on top of one another. In that room, information storage was much more important than the occupant. That meant Kopsin was left with only a small desk shoved into a corner, an armless chair beside it, usually with a pile of papers on it.

In the end, Kopsin talked the rabbi out of taking a position in "the bellies" immediately. He convinced the rabbi to hold off until the newfound zeal had spread far enough to show up in the prices offered for frozen pig carcasses to be delivered three or six months hence (called "futures contracts"). If the price broke out above "the resistance line," however, the strategy was to jump in whole hog with both feet.

Without a word of introduction, Kopsin, his shoulders hunched like an old man's, slid a book of charts in front of the seated Zyg (the pile of papers moved to the floor) and began to lecture like a biblical scholar who had traded the Talmud in for the writings of Edwards and McGee. His eyes bounced back and forth between the black rims of his glasses as he pointed to one chart, then to another. Every time he coughed, the black moles on his pale cheeks jumped up and down convulsively as if snared by a fish hook. Mr. Cliffy was right. At first glance, and even on subsequent glances, the health of Kopsin T. Shurtz made modern medicine seem completely impotent.

"Look at this. Perfect head-and-shoulders," he'd say. Or, "See this lovely rectangle breakout. And here's what an ascending triangle looks like."

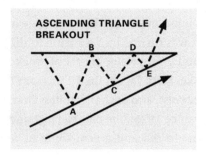

"And look at the Valley Tires pattern. Ever see a more beautiful, beautiful ascending triangle? Is that not what we all hope for in life – basically an ascendance with all the ups and downs. 'The Valley' breaks forty bucks and no question it's on its way to sixty. The volume's there and everything. Look at the pickup in trading. Most people just draw the lines and ignore the volume. Big mistake. Moves in either direction need an increase in trading for confirmation. Nothing in this world is more beautiful than an 'ascending triangle' fulfilling its promise. Nothing."

"That's good to know, Mr. Kopsin," Zyg said as if he understood.

"The only person who calls me Mr. Kopsin is my mother's cleaning lady. I'm good with just Kopsin." He slid his chart book to the other side of his desk. "Mr. Cliffy tells me you've got a union with a pension fund in trouble. Mind you, they wouldn't be the first. Or the last." Kopsin reached for a Kleenex. "Unions, they usually want shares in their employers' companies so they can get in on the gravy train. That's the dumbest thing they can do. They need to diversify. The company could get wiped out and so would their jobs – and their pension fund."

The Back Office at Sutton's would have described Kopsin as taciturn. Here, with a congregation of one, with a potential convert before him, he turned his paper-smothered desk into a pulpit. He paused only to cough his sputter cough and shove Kleenexes into his face, all the while chanting his stock market gospel and hoping his listener might see the light.

"When everybody thinks the market's going nowhere but down, I love it. You have to do your research. You have to read what everybody's saying. Charts aren't everything. You have to do your homework. Right now everybody is so negative you'd think the sky had fallen in. Has to be the bottom."

"How can you be sure?"

"Good question. Great question. Truth is, I can't be. What I'm really doing is guessing. Nobody really knows. Nobody on The Street has any idea really of where this market, or that stock, is going next. But we get paid very handsomely to pretend we do. In truth, we're just a bunch of shamans. I mean, how can you know the future? It's bound to be filled with events we never even thought of."

The U.S. market, as measured by the Dow Jones Industrial Index, had hit a new high in August 1987. Then, in October, it fell as if from a high-wire act. One day alone it dropped 22 percent. Some foreign markets fell even more. To most people on The Street, a meltdown like that meant only one thing: the end of the world.

A group of prominent economists gathered in Washington, D.C., and predicted market turmoil for the next decade. Even old-timers like the founders of IED Securities got so disturbed they quit the investment business for good. Several reps/producers at Federal Wealth put their houses up for sale. And His Worship and the other board members at the Horsemen's Protective Society, who knew little or nothing of the ups and downs of stock markets, discovered their pension fund had taken what The Street calls a bath. A very large and not very warm bath.

Just after lunch the next day, Zyg met again with Kopsin.

"You want a quick opinion?" Kopsin asked.

"Can we help them?"

"Somebody should go to jail for this." Kopsin slapped the four-page statement he was holding. "The guy has thrown in just about every new issue Federal's come out with in the past three years. Me? I wouldn't recommend any one of them, not one, not even to my worst enemy. They're all down. A couple are semi-okay, I guess, but most are absolute crapola." The word *crapola* sounded strangely informal for Kopsin. "Not only that, in a down market like we're in, nobody wants junk like this. They won't even buy the good stuff." Kopsin perused the statement again, leafing back and forth, saying not a word, just snivelling. "It takes time to heal something as badly screwed up as this is."

"What'll I tell them?"

"First, we have to cauterize the portfolio. Stop the bleeding. We sell whatever we can get a decent price for and then buy things more likely to move up when the market turns. In short, take our lumps and move on. That is a very painful process, very painful. But it's the only way. If I'm right, things will look better in five or six months."

"Five or six months?"

"With luck."

"With luck? I can't tell the guys at the society they'll need luck. They know all about luck. They're horse people. They live with luck morning, noon, and night. They know one thing – luck is something you can't count on. Not for love or money."

"The unfortunate thing here is stocks don't go up or down on my say-so. It would be nice if they did, but they don't. We have to rely on the goodwill of others. If the others want to buy stocks, we're in luck. Otherwise, we're not. Nothing good can happen until people get back into a buying mood."

"The society just wants their money back."

"They will get it back. They'll get it back, sure as shooting. Just can't say when."

■ ■ ■

Every Monday morning Sutton's branch manager, Marty Pursutto, the man in charge of hiring and firing reps, asked Zyg to step into his office.

"One thing's sure, my friend, you have not a hope in hell of making a decent living down here with that bunch of bank-huggers you got yourself stuck with. And you know what? You're going to have to teach those folks how to take a little risk. Buy a little something today, you know, and sell it a few months down the line. Make 10, 20 percent, maybe 30. Those government bonds your folks adore won't make them any real money. Not after taxes and inflation. And you know what, my friend? Those bank stocks they like to hold on to forever won't make them rich, either. If you can't get your people to take on a little risk, there's no goddamn way they'll ever make any real dough, and if they don't make any real dough, neither will you. And if you don't, we don't. And that's not good."

"I'm working on something," Zyg said. "I've got a pretty good prospect."

Marty leaned toward Zyg, "That's what you new guys always say. But with your permission may I ask you a simple question?"

"Sure."

"You trying to blow smoke up my ass?"

"Kopsin and I are working on a big account. I've got a really great chance at it. Even Mr. Cliffy thinks so."

"Okay, suit yourself, buddy. We'll see. But take a look at this guy in the paper this morning. Whistling Joe Brakey. Everything he touches turns to goddamn gold. Look, even an old abandoned asbestos mine." Marty threw the newspaper across the desk. "The Brakeys of this world get filthy rich, sure, but along the way they make others rich. Not like bankers. Bankers only make bankers rich. Joe's got this new property in Peru. Looks really, really good. You get your clients in something like that, they could make a shitload. And, of course, if they do, you do, too."

Zyg picked up the paper without replying.

"Let's get something straight. You're not down here to make it a better world for everybody. You're down here to make it a better world for Zyg Adams, right? If that's not so, my friend, you've come to the wrong church. And we both need to know the answer to that, one way or another, soon. Mr. Cliffy's not bankrolling you forever."

Then Marty switched to inspiration. "You know, if you stopped with all that university stuff and instead put your nose to the grindstone here, a guy like you could be in the 5-C Circle in no time. No reason you couldn't find dozens of High Net people at the track. There must be tons of them up there. I mean, they don't call it the sport of kings for nothing. Maybe you could find an accountant or a lawyer or two who'd refer you business."

■ ■ ■

Every Tuesday Kopsin would review the society's account. There was always something to buy or sell as he feathered old stocks out and brought new ones in. These were, however, relatively small trades. The commissions didn't offset Sutton's regular paycheques.

"We're making progress," Kopsin continued to say. "We'd have made more if we'd bet bigger on the oils, but the market's not like playing the ponies. Gentle moves work best. If you try to make a killing, the first thing to get killed usually is you."

Zyg phoned His Worship for approval of any changes Kopsin suggested, and His Worship merely listened and replied, "Do what you think is best." But he didn't sound at all relaxed or comfortable. And he had started smoking again. Still, he must have gained some confidence in Zyg. Otherwise, why would he have given Zyg's name to the Shybert Boys (two brothers and a sister)? The Shyberts had just sold their farming operation north of the city. They sold everything: stables, the horses, the barn, the indoor riding ring, and a hundred and fifty-four acres of land, everything except the homes on small lots severed from the main farm, one where the younger brother lived and the other where the older brother intended to.

On three different evenings, Zyg rented a car and drove the twenty-five miles from Sutton's office downtown out to the farm. The meetings took place in the old-fashioned farmhouse with its gabled roofs and red brick walls edged with buff-coloured quoins and a front entrance that was never used. As soon as Zyg's car reached the end of the long driveway lined with maple trees, the barking of the reception committee – two black retrievers and a honey-coloured collie – began. Only after a half-dozen threats, chastisements, and instructions to "hush up" did the reception committee quiet down and retreat to baskets at the far end of the kitchen/boardroom. Despite all the cooking that must have gone on in that kitchen over the decades and the thousands of food particles that must have lodged their way into the walls and ceiling, the dominant odour by far was that of wet dog.

The brothers, their wives, the accountant, and on one occasion, a lawyer, who didn't answer a question without a thirty-second pause, even if you just asked him the time of day, assembled in the kitchen/boardroom along with the dogs. The sister, Joan-ellen, a one-third owner of the farm, had gone off to Europe to compete in three international riding shows. Her interests were represented by the lawyer.

The older Shybert brother was tall, thin, straight-backed, and most of the time, very straight-faced. His pudgy young brother was experiencing marital difficulties at the time. The week before, his wife found a MasterCard receipt from a motel in the next township where Ken was marketing the Shybert farm's stud services. (As big brother Bill put it, "the bugger was supposed to be out selling semen, for Christ's sake, not sowing it.") The young brother had about as much to say in the meetings as the hushed-up participants asleep in their baskets.

The manager of the local bank came out once to talk about letting his bank manage the account. But the Shyberts hadn't forgotten that bank's refusal to help them through a dry summer eighteen years earlier. Only a small amount of operating capital was left with the banker. Two million dollars for each Shybert was transferred to Sutton Securities, for the brothers all of it designated for investments with no risk attached and that meant strictly bonds issued by the Government of Canada.

When Marty saw that, he went through the roof. "You're just an order taker, Adams. You finally get a couple of decent accounts, but what? Nobody's going to make any decent dough from them. You gotta get those people to pay for your advice. What good's building up a book of customers if they won't buy anything you can make a buck on?"

It looked as if Zyg might get another account thanks to His Worship when a call came in from a steward at Local 721 of the Ironworkers of America, but that fell through.

"You let accounts like that get away, no way you'll ever make The Circle. And, by the way, you be sure to give those farmers a good haircut on the government bonds. You spent one helluva lot of time bringing them in. What I'm saying is if you can't get your production up, my friend, you're in the wrong church as I've told you. This place is strictly for believers. In short, you gotta make them have faith in you, Adams, or you'll never be a big producer. Never."

I've always found it interesting that The Street likes to talk about what it does as "production." At the end of the day in most economic activities, if you produce, you have something to show for your efforts. It could be a chair, a car, a house, a field of swaying wheat, a lump of coal, something you can get your hands on, or at least, touch or use. What Marty meant by "production" was nothing more than a shuffling of numbers – the number of shares or bonds moved from one account to another. At the end of a rep's day there was nothing to see, nothing to smell, taste, or feel. It involved no materials, no aches, no pains, and really no sweat.

Doesn't it strike one as an almost fraudulent use of language to take a word like *production* and apply it to an activity in which hardly none of the same characteristics apply? Toby Williams over at *The World of Finance* thought so. In his "Frequently Unanswered Questions" column, he called it a "cheap metaphor."

Contrast that word usage to, say, the old days at Sutton before the 5-C Circle when the term *Big Dogs* was applied to reps who brought in the most revenue. Big Dogs was a genuine metaphor: those reps barked at everybody all day long, wolfed down their food at lunch, and had to be let out twice a day at the very least.

Besides, if "production" was really what Sutton was all about, why wouldn't the firm call its premises a plant instead of an office? Or, would a funeral director at Pluman's boast about his (or her) production with: "Hey, guess what? I buried six 'pre-needs' this week!"

But Marty wanted production. "Now that you got those new clients, you gotta get close to them. Or you'll spend the rest of your working life cold-calling. How do you get close? Easy. Solve their problems. If their dog needs a vet, find a vet. If their nephew is a dope fiend, find a good drug counsellor. If they're worried about what to get the wife for an anniversary, courier 'em a gift catalogue. Be the go-to guy, not just for investments but for advice about anything. Make them think you care.

"Ever hear of Janie Frost-Sprocket from Houston? She lived next to some famous surgeon. I forget his name. One day, way back, one of her really good clients developed a serious kidney problem. Janie got the client an appointment with her neighbour, the surgeon, who performed a transplant. I'm talking back in the 1960s when they were unheard of. And the best part of the story is that instead of losing a good client, Janie had one for life."

And Marty Pursutto would argue there's always something for clients to buy or sell. It might be something like shares of LookSmart Apparel not snapped up from the prior week's new offering. It didn't matter that one highly regarded hedge fund manager was quoted in Halvert Tulvin's column in *The World of Finance* as saying that LookSmart had about as much chance of turning a profit in the next decade as a hoop-skirt manufacturer. Marty would suggest buying the shares even if Street scuttle had it that LookSmart's Christmas line was far from flying off the shelves of the big fashion stores in town like Bolts.

"You going to worry about Bolts's inventory more than ours? You want us to hold a Boxing Day sale for all our leftover LookSmart shares? Let's get something straight right now. Sutton doesn't do not-for-profit. If our clients want our care and concern, they gotta let us make some dough."

Stated in logical terms, Marty's argument went something like this: *If profitable, we can deliver our clients care and concern. If not, they'll end up in the hands of sleazeballs over at Federal.*

"It's in the client's best interest to let us make a decent living" was another way Marty phrased it. Or, "If we can't make a decent living at what the fuck we do around here, we might as well get a job with the Salvation Army."

In other words, nothing exceeded "production" in importance.

Consider a very short list of Street sins:

- Late trading.
- Insider trading.
- Spinning.
- Soft-dollar payments.
- File-room sex (less frequent now with electronic storage).
- Pay-to-play.
- Bid stuffing.
- Wash trading.
- Rebating.
- Spoofing (and layering).
- Scalping.
- Front running.
- Pump-and-dump.
- Account churning.
- Egregious conflicts of interest.
- Embezzlement.
- Out-and-out fraud.
- Theft.
- **PRODUCTION INSUFFICIENCY.**

Of that very truncated list, which sin would you guess brings on The Street's disdain to the degree that would make the phallic variety seem like a sabbatical in Disneyland?

No matter the economic climate – prosperity or recession, markets trending upward happily or sagging frighteningly lower – reps must produce. That was the natural order of things on The Street. If violated, then a case of "production insufficiency" arose and the new rep's honeymoon was over.

Friendly chatter with fellow reps readily available before vanished. Questions formerly answered promptly became inconvenient, and days passed before a response came back. Even the Back Office (the Untouchables in a brokerage firm's caste system) put up obstacles, citing industry regulations or corporate policies never mentioned before. Invitations for a beer after work disappeared. Whereas the rep might have once felt welcome at Marty's weekly sales meeting, he was now made to feel like the advance party of an Ebola epidemic.

Zyg decided he couldn't afford the time taken to trek all the way out to his old rooming house near the racetrack. Instead, he rented a three-hundred-and-fifty-square-foot bachelor apartment on the seventeenth floor of a mixed-use building ten blocks north of Sutton's offices.

From the previous tenant, he bought the old furniture, including a fold-out bed, two straight-backed parson's chairs, and a small black-and-white television that operated with rabbit ears. The only things he added in the main room were framed pictures of Secretariat and Northern Dancer, and in the bathroom he put up a poster for the 1978 Paris-Dakar Auto Rally.

Most of his meals consisted of fast food from places nearby (at least once a week he "dined with the Colonel" at the nearby KFC franchise), or from frozen pizza and a head lettuce bought from the supermarket in the concourse of his building. Once a week he picked up a six-pack of beer. Local bars were out of the question, except for an occasional trip out to the Wild Goose Tavern, his old haunt near the racetrack, a reward for completing some stage of his M.B.A. Zygmunt hated the apartment. For one thing, it was too far away from the Goose to bring overnight guests.

Some weeks Zyg had to cut out even the beer. His cold-calling brought in a couple of clients with reasonably sized accounts. That helped. Sometimes it's difficult to see that the ups and downs of life might be part of a larger, ascending trend. What caused the breakout for Zyg was the youngest of the Shybert Boys, Joan-ellen, the sister.

■ ■ ■

Shortly after her nineteenth birthday, Miss Shybert married a veterinarian and adopted his last name, Maloney. To help ends meet, she took a part-time job with *Horse, Farm and Field*, writing what was really a gossip column, much of the content identified as pure fiction. She soon became labelled as "Joan-e Baloney." She even began to sign her thank-you notes "Joan-e."

Her one-third interest in the Shybert farm, two divorces, and widowhood helped make her a "High Net." She owned a hundred-and-twelve-acre farm where she trained "dressage" horses, which she took twice a year to competitions along the Eastern U.S. Seaboard or to Europe, mostly Germany. Unlike her brothers, she was a "High Net" not afraid of risk. Kopsin designed a portfolio for her that from the very first day swelled as if on growth hormones.

As is often the case, her considerable assets gave her a considerable number of strong opinions:

- "No artist in this country alive today can paint with William Willard Rumble – I don't care what you say. Only one word describes William Willard's works and that word is *awesome*."

- "The best sushi in town? The New Nagasaki. Next question."

- "Patricia Walters made one great movie, *Light Not the Night*. Everything since has been an utter disaster. I wouldn't go to a flick of hers on a free pass."

- "I've come to realize our friend Cliffy Sutton is quite frankly, was quite frankly, and always will be quite frankly a two-bit crook. The finest moral compass in the world couldn't keep our Cliffy on the straight and narrow for more than half an hour. You know where that huge gap in his front teeth came from? Lying."

- "What good is money, pray tell, if you don't know how to have fun?"

- "You take the Chicky Glickermans of this world. All they do is feed you financial BS. He built his business claiming he cares more about your well-being than his own. Not even the Grimm brothers could come up with a fairy tale that good."

- "If you don't get to Oaxaca in this life, pray you don't miss it in the next."

- "Zyg Adams is the best broker I've ever had. Most of my second husband's so-called friends were brokers. They couldn't hold a candle to Zyg. You know why? He cares. He cares a lot. Zyg trained as an accountant and he knows his stuff. Best of breed. No question. No question whatsoever. Besides, with that little-boy smile of his, you feel you're the one who should be giving the advice. And when I practise my German on him, he never laughs."

Such utterances Joan-e Baloney presented not as mere opinions but rather as statements of immutable facts – unchanging, immutable facts (a trait, Kopsin claimed, prevalent in most of The Street's investment commentary). Within six weeks of becoming one of Zyg's clients, she referred two close friends and an ex-sister-in-law.

In time, other friends of Joan-e's began to call. Not once did Zyg have to ask clients for names of their friends or business associates (though Marty always insisted asking for referrals was the expressway to the 5-C Circle). Zyg sent flowers or a bottle of Veuve Cliquot or tickets to a play at the Royal Alexandra to anyone who referred a client. And Zyg always said thank you for any business he got. Always. And he always did what he said he would do. Always.

And Zyg never made a move in the market without Kopsin's assent. They developed a close business relationship. Kopsin loved Chinese food. At least once a month they had lunch around the corner at Guy Ding's to talk about the market. Its upward climb in those days and Kopsin's discipline worked magic. The contentedness of Zyg's clients quietly grew along with their wealth.

Money opens doors, true. Nothing, however, opens doors like the ability to make other people money. Zyg began to get invited to one event after another. Cocktail parties here, horse shows there, small dinner parties thrown in elegant homes or at "in" restaurants. Zyg cut his cold-calling to one night a week but held on to it mostly to keep himself in shape (the one bit of useful advice from Chicky was: in life you can never get enough training in rejection). Zyg had found his niche market, not a charity or a religion, as Chicky had suggested, but more a quasi-religion of those that, for one reason or another, had great faith in horses.

With Joan-e embedded in his marketing program, with the Horsemen's Protective Society as a client and an endorser, with Kopsin's acuteness and with ten- or twelve-hour workdays (plus that natural little-boy grin), how long would it be before Zyg's "production" broke above the resistance line of $800,000 in a twelve-month period and he got circumscribed by Sutton's 5-C Circle?

Four years and eight months.

"Never in doubt," Marty told the Back Office.

1991

Zygmunt's ascent of Bay Street had taken him far from his early dismal, disinfectant days in the New World as assistant head dishwasher in the cafeteria next to the backstretch of Woodbine Racetrack. Thanks to Mr. Cliffy, Zyg had leapfrogged over the position of head dishwasher to broker-trainee, then to broker, then to "productive" broker, and finally, to another pinnacle – a member in good standing of Sutton's 5-C Circle.

In a short speech near the end of the dinner party he threw at Thrace's to celebrate his thirty-first birthday, Zyg admitted luck helped him to carve out a life far better than he had any right to expect. "I'm at home on The Street," he said. "It's like I lived right around the corner all my life."

Instead of a washer of soiled dishes for the meals and coffee breaks of people who to speak frankly waited on horses, Zyg now sat on the other side of the table with people waiting on him. On Sundays, instead of lurching along a clogged highway on a crowded bus to get to the track, he now scooted out in his velvet red metallic Porsche 944 Turbo S (zero to sixty miles per hour in 5.4 seconds). He'd drive to the stable area, park, and drop into the cafeteria for a quick lunch and to say hello to the head dishwasher and any other acquaintances around that day.

Then he would walk over to the stables to visit with his equine friends in their stalls, munching away on hay or stamping their hooves and wiggling their bodies impatiently. He was an owner now, a shareholder in a syndicate of three stunning fillies trained by Rudy Lamont, Woodbine's leading trainer in 1989 and 1990. If Rudy had one weakness in selecting yearlings to train, it was to favour beauty over speed (a preference that never interfered in Zyg's choice of an overnight companion at the Wild Goose). Zyg would talk with the grooms and hot walkers of his "investments," gathering whatever intelligence he could for his wagers later that day.

Then he'd get back in his car, drive around to the grandstand side, and leave the Porsche and a fat tip with a valet after extracting a promise not to park other cars too close. Next, on his way over to the General Admission stand, he'd pick up a copy of the *Daily Racing Form*, watch a couple of races with Lance and His Worship, and then, after fastening his membership pin, slip up to the Members' area. Occasionally, he brought a date along but that took away the time spent handicapping the horses or from the number of people he could get around to. In this new life, the contact list in his little black book grew every day.

After a day's races, there would be dinner, often at Thrace's or some place around the corner from the penthouse apartment he rented at 120 Bloor Street West, just a half block from Bay Street, on the city's fashion boulevard, Cartier, Tiffany, and Chanel all within a two-minute walk.

When they were finished with dinner, the partiers invariably moved on to Zygmunt's for a nightcap and to hear his latest jazz CDs. Once the guests left, Zyg introduced to his date of the evening the subject of horse breeding – "covering" in equestrian talk. With that kind of talk and ample wine, how far away could the hay be?

When Zyg's "production" numbers climbed, Marty began to address him as "pal." The expression "bank-huggers" disappeared from their conversations. And the Monday morning dyspeptic interrogations ceased. Both his M.B.A. and the gold key chain with its plastic fob with the St. Bernard were awarded to him in the same year.

What would it be like to be a pharaoh with no cares about the after-life? What would it be like to be a kamikaze pilot in training, knowing he'd never get assigned a final mission after the second (and senseless) atomic bomb fell on Nagasaki? What would it be like to be the Sun King in France with unlimited tax revenue? In the ambience of Sutton Securities, not much different than being in the 5-C Circle.

You had your own office. You no longer had to listen to the incessant cackle of your peers (mind you, you could miss out on the odd "good investment idea"). Coffee and muffins were served to you at 10:30 each morning, tea and cookies at 3.00. Even close friends trying to reach you on the phone, if not recognized right off as customers, went through a detailed process of identification to make sure no unwanted party inter-fered with the serious work before you. The endless filing of paperwork was dealt with by others. The group's secretary opened and sorted the mail, made all your luncheon arrangements, making sure, of course, you got a preferred table. For the clients with more complicated needs and who might not like noisy restaurants, she arranged a catered lunch in the boardroom, the lighting appropriately adjusted. Another thing when you were in The Circle, you could blow your stack as Chicky did twice a week, and nobody thought any the worse of you. You, with your circumscribed existence, you, a big producer, deserved every privilege known to mankind. Even Chicky seemed friendlier.

■ ■ ■

"I can't believe I'm saying this, Harvey," Zygmunt said at the Bay Street Squash + Fitness Club. "I came here with nothing. Nada! Didn't have a kettle to piss in. And now I make more dough than I ever dreamed of. Not that I can hold on to much of it. But you know what? I want out. I don't want to do this anymore."

"Out of what?" Harvey Markson asked.

"The courier business."

Harvey picked up the dice on the backgammon board. "You know what? I think we should talk. Losing at squash is one thing, but it sounds like you're losing your mind, too."

Zyg and Harvey hadn't known each other that long. Only two years earlier Mrs. Avogadro, the cleaning lady they shared, suggested the two men meet, and they did in 1989. They became friends, though complete opposites – one cautious, the other with a tendency to be reckless.

And as far as I could tell, they saw their friendship from entirely different perspectives: Zyg considered himself a mentor; Harvey saw himself as the father confessor of an adventurer who thought fate had in store for him only favourable outcomes.

Harvey worked with Rupert H. Winkes, considered by many the best mind on Bay Street. And while Harvey could analyze financial statements inside and out and extract all kinds of vital information about a company's ability to generate profits and profit margins, he was, in Zyg's opinion, unbelievably naive about how seekers of wealth went about seeking it.

Shortly after they met, Zyg joined Harvey's sports establishment, the Bay Street Squash + Fitness Club (known as "The Racquets" and often, unfortunately, confusing Street people as to whether the conversation was about sports or business). The two men had set up a regular Tuesday noon squash match followed by lunch and backgammon.

"Roll the dice, will you, Harv?" Zyg said, taking a sip of beer. "I've got to get back to the office before sundown. You don't know what I do for a living really. You think you do, but you don't. I uncover people who have dough to invest. Right? I ask a few questions. Like how much have you got? What do you want it to do for you? Then I come back to the office and tell Kopsin what they told me. And Kopsin tells me what to tell them. So then I go back and tell the people what Kopsin told me to tell them. They say okay. Then I come back and tell Kopsin okay. And that's it. That's my job.

"That's all I do. I'm just a courier. Only difference between me and some kid on a bike is I don't have to fix flat tires or risk my goddamn neck in traffic. If I could think like Kopsin or loved charts the way he does, I might learn how to make some sense out of all the information he takes in. But reading all that crap about what the market did last month and what it did for the past fifty years and what it's going to do in the next month bores me to – what's the expression? – bores me to ..."

"Tears."

"Right. If I have trouble sleeping, you know what I do? I pick up *The Economist*. Sound asleep in five minutes."

"What the hell would you do with yourself?" Harvey asked. "Get back into dishwashing? That'd be a sound career move."

"I seem to understand businesses a helluva lot better than I understand stocks. I'm getting into mergers and acquisitions."

"You must be kidding. That's a killer sport. It's feast or famine. You work on a deal for months and months, then the day before closing the buyer gets cold feet or his mother-in-law invites him to Naples for the weekend and the whole thing blows up. You never worry about financial security, Zyg, but, man, that's economic bungee jumping. Most guys can only do it for a few years before they burn out. And then they're the long periods where you don't make a dime."

"I'm working on a couple of deals right now – small ones – and they're going okay. I told you about the one with Eddie Murkas and his school bus line. Chip Logan, here at the club, wants to sell his security alarm firm. I know I make good dough as a courier, true enough. But the do-a-deal business is fun. You get to use your noggin. That's what I like. It's not the same old thing day in and day out. Every deal is different. Do a couple of good deals and you're set. With my M.B.A. under my suspenders, shouldn't I do something a little more creative than run errands all goddamn day long?"

"What about your clients?"

"I got a guy, a really good guy, starting next week. Mr. Cliffy's agreed to my new arrangement. I just got to make sure this guy can look after the clients. It'll take a few months, maybe even a year or more, to break him in."

With a flourish, as if signing the Treaty of Versailles or autographing a widely acclaimed new novel, Zyg stopped talking for a second and scribbled a *Z* and an *A* enclosed within a circle on the lunch chit, an obligation of the loser of that day's squash match. "I don't know," Zyg continued. "You know when I do deals, everything seems to fit together. I love the competition. Maybe it's from all the practice I get with women. I'm a negotiator. That was my best subject in my M.B.A. When I get tired of Bay Street, I'll work for the United Nations and help get peace treaties signed. But when it comes to deals, I'm a natural."

Of course, with Zyg's ascent came all the accoutrements of wealth except a wife. Many a time he confessed: "Never, never do I want to find myself that dependent on another human being for my happiness. I tried that once. Still hurts, I swear. Unless a guy can't wait to have kids, the best time to marry is when you're eighty. And that's not so bad an age to try fatherhood on, either. Gets folks talking about you. That's good. You want people talking about you. That's how you can tell you're alive."

Even non-uxorious expenses – rent, food, club memberships, cars, repairs, entertainment, clothes, donations, taxes, horse syndications, bets on horses too slow, flyers on investments that stalled in mid-air or before they even got off the ground – all had a price that riddled Zyg's monthly bank statements with overdrafts and overdraft charges. And even though he now had to give most of the benefits of his "production" to his replacement at Sutton, Zyg didn't alter his lifestyle.

■ ■ ■

Had it not been for Ronnie Blester, better known on The Street as The Pirate (a name awarded early in his career when he briefly wore a patch over an infected eye, but one given greater currency after his first two real-estate deals ended in bankruptcy), Zyg might have received a call or two from his bank manager to come down for a chat. Perhaps a friendly chat. Perhaps not.

The Pirate was the founder of the Canadian Development & Investment Corporation (CDIC), had latched on to the big-box mall concept, and had never let go, building giant malls in the suburbs of Toronto and Vancouver and in two rural Albertan communities that showed signs of sustainable growth. Initially practising law, The Pirate specialized primarily in real-estate litigation and seemed able to get around municipal bylaws as if driving on a six-lane bypass. On any weight scale, his six foot two height and his outsized stomach would have registered two hundred and fifty pounds or more. It was weight he never hesitated to throw around. His light blue eyes would have seemed enchanting in a woman's face; in The Pirate's, however, I always thought they intimated a lack of trustworthiness.

Separated from his wife of four years the month before, Ron the Pirate showed up as Joan-e Baloney's date for the one-hundred-and-fourth running of the Breeders' Stakes. In the sixth race, both he and Zyg bet on the same horse and lost. And then they lost again in the Stakes race when their choice, a chestnut brown colt, Wiser in Winter (by Platonic Lover out of Snowdrift), chose not to run a lick from start to finish. A kinship struck up between the two men. At Thrace's that night Joan-e seated Ron next to Zyg. The whole evening they talked business, ignoring everybody else, Ron doing most of the talking.

The following Monday afternoon a copy of Andy Wainright's *Picking Winners: A Horseplayer's Survival Guide* arrived at Zyg's office with a note that read:

> *We need all the help we can get!*
> *Ron*
>
> *R.W. BLESTER CDIC*

On Wednesday a formal invitation to join Ron and Joan-e at a gold sponsor's table for the Have a Heart Gala arrived.

> *Hope you and a lady friend will join our table. Fabulous wine auction!*
> ***Ron***
>
> **R.W. BLESTER CDIC**

And the day after the gala came a phone call from Ron's secretary to set up a lunch meeting in a private room at the Museum Club, just around the corner from Zyg's penthouse, with Ron and CDIC's chief financial officer.

However admirable CDIC's rapid growth – and its growth had "skyrocketed" according to *The World of Finance* – its need for capital had grown faster, and with Blester's divorce on the horizon, faster yet. Sheardon-Cassidy had submitted terms for the underwriting and considered the deal a *fait accompli*. And, as the story goes, when a couple of weeks later Ron told its chairman, Eldred "Piggy" Donnis, that he had accepted Zygmunt Adams's proposal over Sheardon's, there came the usual response.

"Zygmunt? Zygmunt who? Zygmunt Who-the-Hell?" Eldred demanded, his voice high-pitched with anger.

But few people got to burn Eldred twice. He knew exactly what to do. Some three months after the CDIC deal was put to bed, Zygmunt Who-the-Hell moved up The Street from Sutton to the fiefdom of Eldred "Piggy" Donnis, chairman, chief executive officer, president, commander-in-chief, or as some put it, the head hog of Sheardon-Cassidy International.

Or as Zyg later put it, more simply and succinctly, "Sir Oink."

1993

"I had them rush-rush your cards," Eldred Donnis told Zyg. "Got to get things the hell moving around here. Or, believe me, we'll be in trouble. Real trouble."

It was Zyg's second day on the job, a few minutes after four o'clock, and the market had just closed.

"I go away for a month and everybody around here falls asleep. That's what bull markets do? They lull people into sleep. The stupid bugger who had your job, after twenty years in this business still thinks – still! – school keeps forever. Forever! Jesus! With markets that's the most stupid goddamn thought you can ever put in your head."

Eldred swung his chair around and opened the drawer of the mahogany credenza behind him. "Never, never trust markets. Not for a second. The minute you do they punch you in the nose. And what happens then? People wander around like they're hung over. You know why I buy this Scotch?" He reached into the drawer and brought out a bottle of Glenfiddich. "For taste? Not particularly. To show off? Uh-uh. Zero hangover. Zero." He tilted the neck of the bottle toward Zyg.

"No thanks, Mr. Donnis."

Eldred poured the golden-brown liquid into a low cut-glass tumbler, barely leaving room for an ice cube. "Your first job is to get these lazy buggers around here up off their asses. We need new clients. When the goddamn market tanks, and it will – you can count on it – you need a big fat buffer of extra clients. We need more retail investors, we need more institutions, more corporations – whatever – doing business with us. We have to be topped up, like my drink." He poured several drops of water into his drink from a pitcher on the credenza. "Topped up with clients because a lot of them are going to lose money and leave.

"You know what your predecessor wanted to do? Wanted to run some glitzy goddamn advertising campaign. Print. TV. Radio. Whatever. Advertising is money out the window. All we need is our people out talking to people. That's better than TV, radio, and newspapers all rolled into one. Last time one of those newspaper ad salesmen talked me into something, the response was so pitiful I got my money back. Never advertised since. Just a waste. Our people out talking to people cost next to nothing."

While Eldred spoke, Zygmunt ran his fingers over one of his new embossed business cards that read: EXECUTIVE VICE-PRESIDENT, BUSINESS DEVELOPMENT. And the name of Sheardon-Cassidy – better known than Sutton's and much more prestigious from long before 1969 – meant a fresh challenge. And Zyg liked that. He liked that a lot.

Eldred Donnis paid his executives well, that's true. As with most things Eldred did, there was a catch. Instead of one job, his executives had more than one. No firm on The Street of any significance had an executive position like Zygmunt's. He was responsible for "wealth management" (making profits from risking other people's money) and manager of mergers and acquisitions (making profits from companies buying and selling one another).

Zyg brought in Nadia Whitall, formerly manager of the most successful women's fashion store in the city, Bolts (referred to by local citizens as "Nuts and Bolts," much in the same way Superior Interiors, the design studio of Harvey Markson's friend, Zuzu Hornfeldt, was always called "Inferiors").

Safe to say, nobody in the city knew more about delivering service than Nadia (though she declined to deliver any to Zyg when he drove her home from Joan-e's dinner party some years before). What he needed was someone who could pick up the morale of Sheardon's reps. Nobody would bring more enthusiasm to the job than little Nadia with her high-wattage energy. Nadia's main message to the reps was: "What you guys deal is not stocks and bonds – it's trust."

Another idea of Zyg's to help turn the culture around was to get some "big producers" to join Sheardon. After two months of on-again-off-again negotiations, Zygmunt lifted out, as you would the first piece of a birthday cake (*snare* was the *The World of Finance*'s term), a whole branch from Federal Wealth.

The "branch" included Arnold "Sunny" Sonblach (a bilingual Montrealer) and the husky-shouldered, six-four Martin "Mega" Hurtz (fluent neither in French nor English, his native tongue). The third member was Toddy Landau (the 1991 club champion at the Port Credit

Lakeside Golf Club). What sold the three was Zyg's insistence that at Sheardon they'd be treated not as bank employees but as full-fledged, out-and-out entrepreneurs. That was the way they saw themselves. And they also liked what they saw on their signing bonus cheques, though Eldred didn't – not one bit.

Sunny Sonblach would say in his deep, solemn voice, phone receiver nestled against his square jaw, "We like Glacial Advances. We like it a ton. Great technology. Great management. Super, super balance sheet. Cash just pours in. Glacial can freeze anything from a gopher to a gazelle. And at half the price of the competition. They'll have fifty facilities by the end of the year. Next year a hundred." Then he'd add, "Talk about investing long-term. I read in *The World of Finance* that frozen meat can stay fresh for twenty thousand years. Their guys are talking strictly North America. Not a word about Asia or the tropics. My point is they've barely scratched their potential markets. Valuation's a tad high, true. I can't deny that. All the same, we think the stock's an easy double in the next twelve to … ten thousand shares? Stock's five-fifty. I even put some in my wife's portfolio. Plenty of room in your margin account. And we haven't even talked about what global warming will do for business. Why not make it twenty thousand?" And after a short pause: "Thanks. 'Preciate that."

Not an "umm," not a "you know," not a moment's hesitation scrambling for the *mot juste*, not one little tremor of doubt overlaid his words. That was Sunny at his best, speaking with all the assurance of a saint after prayer and in such a mellifluous, assured way even skeptical clients dared not ask if the commission was negotiable.

To provide a little background on the triumvirate, in the early 1990s, Federal Wealth opened a new branch in one of the bank buildings on Bay Street, displacing the studios of the very popular Toronto Folk Dance Academy. On the other hand, it meant a bit of good fortune for Sunny et al. They took over not only the space but also the name. From then on, to strengthen their brand, they called themselves The Academy, hoping clients would associate their new name with the school in ancient Greece where, in the fourth century B.C., Plato and Aristotle hung out along with Athena, the goddess of wisdom.

Appearances were important to the Academicians, especially to Sunny and Mega. They dressed the same in blue- or red-striped shirts with white collars, initialled cuffs, large cufflinks, dark ties, and extra-wide suspenders beneath their shoulder-clinging JimSmith© bespoke suits. "In this business, you don't need to be smart, you just have to look smart," Sunny claimed.

And the Academicians bent over backward for clients: tracking down a brown hypoallergenic dog of medium height and not too dark a brown; nailing down opera seats in the orchestra section, not too close to the stage and not twenty-five rows back; finding a house-keeper to come on Wednesdays and every other Friday; or locating ("like yesterday") a top-notch endodontist for the infected tooth of the captain of the Rosedale lawn bowling team.

While other Federal Wealth branches had a mixture of clients, The Academy had only one variety: very profitable. And with scholastic diligence they did everything in their power to keep clients profitable. They would sell clients stock in a new issue (with extra commission built in), open a "margin" account so they could borrow and "back the truck up" on a promising stock, or persuade them on the diversification advantages of long-short hedge funds with fat fees. And when Chinese competition wiped out Matty Brinson's kitchen equipment business and the quarterly production figures showed Mr. Brinson's account barely profitable, with the speed of light it found its way to a junior rep at Federal's main branch.

Ninety-three percent of The Academy's clientele came over from Federal to Sheardon-Cassidy. In the first year, the triumvirate produced well over $4 million in commissions. Chairman Donnis was delighted. And, to boot, just as Zyg had hoped, their presence attracted other "big producers" to Sheardon-Cassidy.

"You work for Sheer Mendacity? Wow! Cool!" might be the sort of clichéd comment you heard in the pub on the concourse level of Sheardon's office building. Job applications poured in. The Street began to award Sheardon larger chunks of all the new bond and stock underwritings.

When the Paris office floundered, Zyg flew over every other month and developed several major accounts with European banks and insurance companies. He travelled the Paris-Frankfurt-Basel-Milan circuit (often accompanied by a demoiselle from Paris) until he stole Jean-Claude Frochet away from Garmeau Frères to run the Sheardon office.

And if some rep showed he couldn't measure up, it was Zyg who broke the news. "Some people are meant for The Street. Some aren't. If you aren't, you'll always feel out of place – like a frog out of breath." Even if the departing employee didn't quite understand Zyg's mangled clichés, he did appreciate the way the matter was handled and left Sheardon without the usual bitterness. Zyg remembered well the pain of production insufficiency.

Nor did Zyg, no matter how busy his schedule, forget Kopsin Shurtz. Time was always found for lunch at Guy Ding's. At one lunch Kopsin commented offhandedly that his charts showed "something awfully fishy" going on at a gold-mining company that had captured all the journalists' attention. Zyg alerted his research department, and Sheardon's clients reduced their positions considerably over the next weeks. When the news came out in 1997 that Bre-X's head geologist had fallen to his death from a helicopter in Borneo, the few shares clients still held were dumped the next day. Soon after it was discovered that the mineral assays had been tampered with and "salted" with gold purportedly shaved from jewellery.

Even those who moved to a different part of the province kept their accounts with Sheardon. How much that had to do with Nadia's "service strategies" nobody could put a number on. What they did know was that the company's monthly financial statements began to look better and better, and that pleased Eldred Donnis no end. He started to boast to people what a smart hire Zyg was.

1998

The doctors diagnosed Eldred Donnis as pre-diabetic in 1998. His wife, Grace, known to her friends as "The Amazer," insisted it was time for him to slow down on his drinking and on his business involvement. It was only natural then for him to appoint his golden-haired boy, Zygmunt Adams, Sheardon's president and chief operating officer. Zyg liked the idea to a point, but in his opinion there was a "flaw in the ointment."

As he followed Harvey Markson out the glass door of the court at Bay Street Squash + Fitness Club, Zygmunt, puffing like a rhino run to ground, said, "Somebody's getting luckier and luckier out there. If I hadn't slipped, I would've had you cold on the last point."

The two men sat at their regular backgammon table in front of court 4, each rubbing his head and neck vigorously with towels. "You know what, Harv? I think I'm going bananas or something. Working for The Pig is no piece of candy. I'll say one thing, though. I don't understand why he has problems with his blood sugar. There isn't one sweet thing about the man. Whenever some poor guy drops a nickel or dime on the floor, Eldred's little hoof shoots out, steps on it, and claims it's his. I don't know why I let him talk me into this job. I turned it down originally, you know. The dough's good, but everything else is wild. I'm getting too old for that kind of crap. You just saw it – I'm not moving around the court the way I used to. And, to tell you the truth, what has me more worried, I'm not moving around in the bed the way I used to."

"Wait a minute, Zyg. I don't know how your sex life's doing these days, but I don't ever remember you being exactly a gazelle on the squash court."

Here was Zyg, risen from assistant head dishwasher to registered rep to the prime mover at Sheardon, talking like that. He had his fast car and a penthouse apartment, rented, mind you; was part owner of three yet-to-show-their-speed horses; and possessed a PalmPilot full of the names of women, half of whom he couldn't put faces to. And in a week he would be able to add to all that the title of president and chief operating officer of Sheardon-Cassidy International.

"I mean, I'll do it for a couple of years, make my potful, and go on to something else. But ever since I accepted The Pig's offer, all the life seems to have gone out of my life."

Harvey moved his backgammon checker forward three spaces. "You really think you could walk away from all that? I don't see you doing that, not in a month of Sundays. Do you see yourself doing that?"

"Last night, Miss Erotica, remember her? A couple of weeks ago at the track? The one whose smile makes Mona Lisa look like she's wearing dentures? Well, I finally got her back to the apartment. Took a lot of work. A lot of work and an unusual amount of patience, something I'm not so good at. It was late, though, and just as I was about to pour her a snifter of my best Armagnac, I remembered – Jesus! – I have a 7:00 a.m. meeting with Eldred. I explained I had to be sharp and went to the kitchen to call a cab for her. When I came back, she was gone. *Disparu*." Zyg rolled the dice. "Any sane man would give his left leg to get her in the sack, and here I'm worrying about Eldred and his stupid goddamn meeting."

"Right leg."

"Work for Eldred and – I mean, Jesus – you can kiss any real life goodbye. No time for anything but the office. And it's not like I'm doing something a hundred other guys couldn't do. When they convinced Eldred he needed to take better care of himself, I just happened to be there."

"You told me you were slowing things down at work. Didn't you tell me you and The Pirate were entering a car rally next week?"

"Yeah, but that's the first weekend I've taken off this year. And what I'd really like to do is get into one of the big international rallies for a couple of weeks. Across Africa or something. And here's another thing that gets to you after a while. Ron's bought this door manufacturer. He wants me to run it. Can you imagine having something at the end of the day you can see and touch like a wooden door? In our business, you break your ass all day and at the end of it, what've you got? A few more bucks and a bunch of numbers." Zyg held his arms wide apart. "And zip else."

"Do you seriously think you'd be happy in a factory?"

Zygmunt ignored Harvey's question. "Let's order lunch. I gotta get back."

■ ■ ■

Later in 1998 the shoe was on the other foot. One evening on his way to a meeting of the Nasagaweya Conservation Association,

Rupert Winkes, Harvey's senior partner and mentor, swerved his Volvo to avoid a startled deer. The car plunged down an embankment and landed upside down on a rock outcrop, its roof smashed tight up against the floorboards.

Control of the investment-counselling firm fell into the hands of Rupert's brother-in-law, a periodontist. In very quick order, the brother-in-law revealed a few shortcomings: he didn't have a clue about finance, not a clue about corporate management, and certainly not a clue about investments. It became a question whether the man had any judgment at all other than bad.

Zygmunt had a lot to say to Harvey about those circumstances. "Harvey, you gotta get your butt the hell out of there. You were in the right place. Now you're in the wrong place at the wrong time. No, I'm wrong. Neither the brother-in-law nor that pseudo-economist he hired should be in charge of anything larger than a mid-sized car wash. Jesus, Harv, come to your senses, Chrissake! There's nothing – not a goddamn thing – you can do to make that place work. Face it, Harvey. The guy's a disaster. Plain and simple. You got a problem and I've got the solution: come over and run our research department."

"Why are you always so sure you know what the hell you're talking about, Zyg? You don't even know the guy." You could tell the strain was getting to Harvey. He rarely got angry.

"Since when did having a few street smarts become a sin, Harv, tell me? Since when?"

But Zygmunt had called things right on. And when the brother-in-law made the economist the chief investment officer, Harvey had no choice but to resign. He had to sue to have the firm buy back his shares, which seven months later yielded him 90 percent of Zyg's lowest guess. Harvey sold his condo and its contents and headed off to a job in London in the late spring of 1999. But the firm in London had formed a hasty merger with a Hong Kong company facing bankruptcy and had put in a hiring freeze. Harvey, jobless and dispirited, and much against his better judgment, accepted Zyg's offer to take over Sheardon's Paris office and help buoy its European operations.

1999

Like Zyg, Bay Street wasn't known for its patience. Three months after Zyg hired his friend Harvey for the Paris office, Eldred didn't like the look of the numbers coming in from Europe. While Zyg was in Lima, trying to land part of a Peruvian government bond issue before going on a long-planned South American car rally, Eldred convinced his Sheardon partners that Europe was beyond hope. Zyg called late in the afternoon of his third day in Lima with an update on the bond deal, but Eldred wasn't listening. "Europe looks terrible," he interrupted.

"Listen to me for once, Eldred. The absolute last thing you want to do at this point is change things around in Europe." Zyg took his time with each word. "You don't want to do that. You need to understand. We just put in place two of the best guys you could find on this whole goddamn planet. You gotta give 'em a chance, for Chrissake. We'll make good dough in Europe.

"The money managers over there are hungry for good ideas. I talk to them all the time. They're not confident about their new euro currency. We have it all over all the U.S. banks. You never know which side of a trade they're on. But you don't build trust in a day. Our manager in London's a gem. A really good, good guy, Eldred. And you know Harvey Markson and all the brainpower he's got – that has to pay off for us. He's been with us – what? – three, four months, and the orders are starting to roll in already. And there'll be other things – deals, acquisitions –"

"But we're losing dough there hand over fist," Eldred broke in, his words sharp. "The euro's nothing but a goddamn pipe dream. I don't bet on pipe dreams. And then, goddamn it, today your friends at Save Your Time, that stupid software company, phoned and asked for more money. Then, on top of that, I get this monthly report from London and the numbers look pathetic. We're making too many mistakes. No use good money coming in one door and going out the other. We gotta make changes."

"What kind of changes?"

"Europe's dead in the water, Zyg. I know you think it will work.

Maybe you're right, if we could wait for goddamn ever. The partners and I aren't willing to put another cent in over there. You might have sold them on it six months ago. Now it's too late. They're fed up to the teeth with Europe."

"They are? Or you are?"

"The Street is cleaning up these days left and right. And that makes me very nervous. You know that. Something's gonna break soon."

"It's all a year 2000 buildup. Tech's way overbought. And you said yourself we need to diversify our clientele. That's why I put all that effort to get London and Paris on stream again. Takes time. Europeans don't rush into things."

"Maybe, maybe. But we should be making a killing before the market goes south."

"We're doing okay. What you're really saying is you're not willing to wait, right?"

"We won't make a nickel in Europe for five years."

Zyg's toned changed. "Eldred, sounds to me like you've dug your hooves – heels – in," Zyg quickly corrected. "Is that what's going on? You've given up on Europe. Is that it?"

"Correct."

"Eldred, after six years you know me pretty well. And you know I can't go along with that. I've made commitments."

"No, I'm just facing facts. Europe is finito."

"Well, I can't just stand by and see my guy in London and my friend, Harvey, get screwed. Sheardon has obligations to them. If you're not willing to live up to those obligations, I've got a suggestion for you."

"What's that?"

"You can take the whole Sheardon-Cassidy shooting match and –"

4
The Zyg Zags

Rest assured, you don't tell the leader of a prestigious Bay Street financial house such as Sheardon-Cassidy International to take his entire enterprise and relocate to a place where only a top-notch colorectal surgeon could find it and expect your future to go unaltered.

Before going on the planned car rally the next day, Zyg emailed Harvey, but to his old address, and some time passed before Harvey got to read it. The message simply said: "Harv, your buddy Zyg had to zag."

Zyg had timed his trip to Lima to coincide with a warm-up for the great Andean Cross-Country Rally (from Lima to Playa del Moro, Argentina). He had arranged to take part as a co-driver. So it wasn't until five days after his instructions to Eldred Donnis that Zyg arrived back in Toronto. He stayed in town only long enough to sell his Porsche back to the dealer, hire a real-estate agent to sublet his condo, and with the help of Mrs. Avagadro, get all his belongings packed in suitcases or boxes and shipped to Vancouver. And, of course, he had lunch with Kopsin at Guy Ding's. The only other person Zyg spoke to during his short stay was Joan-e, who met him at the airport for a drink before his flight. A hotel development of The Pirate's in Vancouver was six months behind schedule and at least a million dollars over its budget. The project needed someone to get it back on track "like pronto as in Toronto."

Though many of Vancouver's inhabitants are escapees, or descendants of escapees, from the Greater Toronto region, many dislike

Toronto because of its arrogance, its disproportional influence on the central government, and its hockey team's relentless pursuit of mediocrity. Many chose to live in Vancouver because of a different set of values: having chosen sky-high mountains and an endless ocean over money-hustling and ever-present impatience.

Like people in most large cities, the residents of Vancouver are in no more of a hurry to include newcomers into their circles than members of Sutton's 5-C into theirs. The city's inhabitants prefer not to have their lives interrupted by strangers, especially ones from "down east."

No matter what Zyg did to get to know people either from business, from the sailing club he joined, or from acquaintances he made at the supermarket or coffee shop around the corner from his apartment, some of whom displayed little reluctance to accompany him to bed, he never felt accepted by the city.

One evening in early spring he sat at the patio bar of the Bayshore Hotel awaiting a prospective companion, admiring the scene in front of him with the harbour, the skyline of the city's downtown, and the mountains beyond. There and then it struck him that he felt more at home with money-hustling, impatience, and athletic mediocrity. The minute he finished a second project for The Pirate he made a beeline for Toronto.

Four years had passed, enough time to have his scandalous exit buried in The Street's memory beneath its many subsequent scandals, especially those that showed up from the dot.com market crash of the early 2000s.

Spring 2003

When Zyg arrived back in Toronto, Sheardon-Cassidy, the country's largest independent brokerage firm, had been acquired and absorbed by Federal Wealth and Great Trust (*The World of Finance* called the deal a merger). By then, both of us (my brother, Roi, and I), who Eldred Donnis had put in charge after Zygmunt left, had resigned from Sheardon.

Eldred and his wife, Grace, had moved to Nassau, thirty minutes by plane from first-rate medical service in Miami. Bon Chance, their country home, site of all the wonderful parties Grace had thrown, was scooped up for more than $6 million. And Joan-e Baloney, Zyg's friend and the client who helped the most to build his practice in his early days at Sutton, had replaced Grace as the city's most important hostess. Harvey Markson had established residence in Bermuda, though he never seemed to be there, orbiting the world like a celestial body, doing deals for the giant QRS Bank, one minute in Hong Kong, the next in Rio and then in Sydney.

Zyg rejoined the Bay Street Squash + Fitness Club but had trouble, or so he complained, finding opponents with the same level of talent as Harvey. He attended the races at Woodbine most Sundays, spending the afternoon with Lance and His Worship, but without the same fervour and enthusiasm of before. Cashing a winning ticket no longer seemed to him like a metaphysical statement on his prospects for the good life. He was forty-three and listless.

"If I had a smile as pretty as yours, the last thing people would see on my face is a frown," Zygmunt said to the woman standing impatiently beside him at the temporary bar set up in Joan-e's dining room. According to the couriered invitation, this evening was: "An Early Salute to Summer: Drinks and hearty hors d'oeuvres. 5:30 to 7:30." It was nine o'clock. Hardly anybody had left.

The woman replied, her frown still in place. "You're Bay Street, aren't you?"

"Could be."

"Once you've worked anywhere near there," the woman said as she looked around the room, more or less ignoring Zygmunt, "you can spot that Bay Street *merde* a mile away."

"You said *merde*. You're French?"

"Very clever. But, no, not really. My father was."

"Would it be impolite to ask your name, *si vous permettez*?" Zyg all but clicked his heels.

"Antoinette."

"Ah, Marie Antoinette?"

73

"No, as a matter of fact, it's Antoinette Mairie. My father had a sense of humour at one time. And it's not Marie, it's Mairie, as in City Hall."

"Well, Madame Mairie, may I ask why you hold us poor Bay Street folk in such low regard?"

"Wrong again. It's not Madame. It's Mademoiselle Mairie. And the lack of regard is based solely on experience. I can't imagine another place on the planet with a greater density of egomaniacs. You people like to say you're in financial services. But, in my opinion, for what that's worth, it would be more accurate to say in financial self-services."

"Hey, you're serious."

"Sell! Sell! Sell! That's all you guys ever think about. Sell. Sell. Sell."

"We're just trying to earn a little pin money."

"Yeah, for your voodoo dolls, I bet."

Mademoiselle Mairie turned to the bartender. "Gin and tonic, please. Mostly tonic. Tiny, tiny bit of gin. One cube of ice, please, Bartender. And a slice of lemon, just a small slice." She then moved to the side of the bar, but still facing Zyg.

Her blue-rimmed glasses seemed intended to fend off any close study of her eyes. She had a freckled, slightly reddish complexion, and when not frowning, a smile that suggested a complete refusal to take seriously anything going on about her. She was a little taller than Zyg, something he usually found attractive.

In the background, just over Antoinette's shoulder, the president of Etobicoke Freight Forwarders, an important client in Zyg's Sheardon days, waved hello. Zyg raised his index finger to signal "I'll be with you in a moment." When he turned back to the bar, Mademoiselle Mairie had left – *disparu* – not to be seen again until a half-hour later walking toward the front door, her hand on the arm of a tall, balding man.

Sent: 06/03/2003 9:45 a.m.
From: zygadams@sympatico.ca
To: hmarkson9077@gmail.com
Subject: Joan-e's Party

Nomad, you missed one great party. You better get back here. Just like the old days. Joan-e outdid herself. She asked me to say hello for her. Hello.

People were still in the pool at midnight when I left – solo. You ever know a woman by the name of Antoinette Mairie? I don't know what the hell she does, but it must be something to do with Bay Street. She looks like a teenager but – whew – she is one tough hombre. She dismissed me like a piece of chopped turkey. Good thing I got all that rejection training at Sutton or she might have hurt my feelings. She's more your type. Come to think of it, you ever come to your senses and return to Toronto, she'd be perfect for you. For me, though, if I never see her again, it would be too soon, way, way too soon. All the same, great party.

Keep in touch,
Zyg.

"Way, way too soon" turned out to be three weeks later.

That particular day, though, had been a terrible one for Zyg. After weeks of early-morning meetings and sixteen revisions to the "term sheet," Ennis Enterprises got cold feet and at the last moment backed out of acquiring Caledonia Geothermal Systems. That deal would have skated Zyg back onside with his banker, no question. And on that day, too, Zyg's car was broken into in the parking garage of his office building. He'd forgotten to lock his car doors, and thieves scratched his dashboard all to hell trying to steal the passenger-side airbag, though without success. They did grab the $2,000 cash kept in the bottom of the glove compartment in anticipation of the electrical grid going down one day.

About four o'clock that afternoon the date he'd invited twenty-four hours earlier left a voice mail, her words so badly slurred it was hard to make out her message, especially with the background bar chatter. The gist of it, however, was that she was sick and tired of being the fallback date in his life, always getting called at the last minute. So she wouldn't be available that particular evening as previously agreed, and what was more, she added the point that if he didn't like that "and was still in the mood to get laid, he could go screw himself."

In turn, he left a voice mail for Joan-e and explained that his date was "a little under the weather, but he would be at the gala that night, though unescorted and perhaps a bit late."

∎ ∎ ∎

"You're Zyg Adams? I had no idea," said the person seated alone at Joan-e's table when he arrived, the other members up dancing or visiting. "Probably shouldn't have listened to Joan and stayed home. She mentioned your name, but it didn't mean anything to me, of course. Besides, Joan is very persuasive."

"Here's a thought. Why not start over?" Zyg held out his hand. "Hello, my name is, um, Zygmunt Adams. And, you are Mademoiselle, um, I believe, Mademoiselle Mairie. A pleasure to meet you in person. *Enchanté*."

"At Joan's party I was running on exhaustion. And mad as hell, too. My father-in-law-to-be had just sold his house to pay off the stupidest loan I ever heard of." Zygmunt didn't catch the part about the house or the loan but did hear "father-in-law-to-be" quite distinctly.

"One of your wonderful Bay Street big producers, you know one of those moral dwarfs who wear ankle-length leather coats and assure you they can set you up in financial heaven, told the man if he wanted to retire before the age of a hundred and eighty, he had to invest more aggressively. He'd just paid off his mortgage with the life insurance payments when his wife died of cancer. First time he'd been out of debt since he started medical school. The man was sixty-three."

"And what happened?"

"You know. A year later the market fell out of bed, of course. My father-in-law-to-be hung in until he couldn't make the margin calls for more money. He has terrific expenses with a stepson in a home. So instead of a nice house to live in, he had to sell and move into a dingy apartment a block from his hospital. The man's a medical researcher. He wouldn't have the foggiest idea about business, much less the stupid stock market."

"What did the broker say?"

"Oh, yes, the broker told my fiancé he was 'very *saw-ree*,'" Antoinette replied, faking a husky voice. "'Terribly *saw-ree*,' in fact. There was, unfortunately, he said, nothing he could do about it. Company rules didn't allow him to. Of course, we know the broker won't have to wait until he's a hundred and eighty to retire. Probably about the same time it would take the dumb bastard to get through high school."

"How about getting legal help?"

"He didn't want to go to court. He didn't have the money, time, or energy for that, he said."

That night I was Joan-e's escort at the Mariachi Gala. When we got back to the table, she said, "Antoinette, you're such a good sport to come along. You know how I hate uneven numbers at a dinner party." She and Antoinette pressed cheeks. "We miss you up at the farm. The horses miss you, and so does my little black poodle who adores you."

"With the wedding and my practice, I'm snowed under these days," Antoinette said. "After the wedding, you'll probably get tired of me coming out to ride. And if that darling little dog of yours ever has another litter, sign me up."

"Speaking of stray dogs, I want you, Zygmunt, on your best behaviour tonight," Joan-e said as she held out her cheek for a greeting kiss. "Antoinette's fiancé's been travelling all over Asia for the past month. Can't be all work and no play for the poor girl. Antoinette, if this reprobate gives you any trouble, you let me know. I know how to deal with him."

"Needn't worry, Joan. I know these Bay Street types. But just to let you know, I have to leave a bit early. I have a client coming in tomorrow at eight."

The other four guests, Beth and Charles (I never did get their last names straight) and Jack and Klemmy Testostero (who I knew well), came back to the table, and Joan-e introduced them around.

"Not until eight?" Zyg said to Antoinette after everybody was seated. "I'll have played my squash game and showered by then."

"I like tennis better."

"Doubles or singles?"

"Doubles."

"You don't get a workout."

"Maybe, but in squash you can get your teeth knocked out. And they're my best feature."

"Doubles is almost as bad as golf. No calories burned."

"I think golf is a marvellous game. It's so nice to get out in the fresh air."

"It's a game for the delusional. If I hadn't six-putted the last four greens, I could have broken a hundred and fifty."

That wasn't a good start to the evening. Not good at all. *Pas du tout.*

Not even a good restart. And from what I could overhear, it didn't get much better the rest of the night.

"I can't agree," said Antoinette after dinner. "I love books. No gadget will ever replace nestling in a big chair with a good book. Not ever."

Or Zyg later on saying something like: "Do you really think we know enough about the weather to make predictions fifty years out? As far as I can tell, those guys have trouble getting the next day right."

When the orchestra played "Feelings" and Antoinette and Zyg got up to dance, they looked as if they were rehearsing for a Baroque ball. And when the peach flambé arrived, they were in the midst of a disagreement about whether poodles made better pets than golden retrievers.

Shortly after Joan-e went off to speak to the gala's convener, Antoinette glanced at her watch and said to Zyg, "Thanks for the evening. I'm going to grab a cab and get along." She held out her hand.

"You kidding? I'm too young to die. Joan-e would have me in front of a firing squad at dawn if I don't see you home. I have to be up early, too."

On the way out, Antoinette blew a kiss to Joan-e across the room, and Zyg waved.

Evidently, when they got to the door of Antoinette's apartment, out of habit, Zyg claimed, he started to give her the usual ritual goodnight kiss on the cheek. But when he swung his head to kiss the other cheek, their lips met squarely on. There was a pause. And then her hand clasped the back of his neck firmly, very firmly.

Before he tiptoed out of the apartment the next morning shortly after six, Mademoiselle Antoinette fast asleep, Zyg wrote on the back of one of his business cards: "Didn't want to wake you. Will call later. Best sleepover ever. *Mille mercis.* Z."

In the early-morning breeze, two yellow parking tickets flapped under the windshield wiper of his Porsche. Zyg took them off and shoved them into his inside coat pocket. As he drove away, all he could say was: "Well! Well! Well!"

■ ■ ■

Since his return from Vancouver, Zyg had been working out of a rented office in a business centre on King Street two blocks west of Bay. After his squash game, shower, and breakfast, he got to his office where an oversized security officer was waiting to quiz him about the break-in of his car the day before. As soon as the two men sat down in Zyg's office on either side of his desk, the phone rang.

"Sorry to bother you, Mr. Adams. I know you asked not to be disturbed. The party on the phone insists. They won't give me a name. Should I tell her to call back later?"

Zyg glanced at the security officer. "Mind if I take a quick call? Sounds important. My aunt just got out of the hospital."

"No problem," replied the guard, who pecked away at his BlackBerry without looking up.

"Zyg Adams," Zyg said to the phone.

"Zyg?"

"Oh, hi, Aunt Sally. You okay?"

"It's not Aunt Sally. It's Antoinette."

"Oh, I'm so sorry to hear that, Aunt Sally. Want me to call you a doctor?"

"No, don't call anybody. Most of all, don't call me. Last night was a huge mistake. Write it off as a one-night stand, will you, please? I must have been a little *grise* from all the wine. Every once in a while my French blood gets the better of me. Please don't call me. I'm getting married in a couple of weeks, for God's sake. Forget it ever happened, Zyg, please. It was a one-night stand. Don't take it as anything more."

"Oh, that sounds awful, Aunt Sally! A migraine?" Zyg raised his voice as if surprised. "I'll get a doctor right over."

"I don't want a doctor. I don't want you to call anybody. Or me. Please. There's nothing further to be said. It was all my fault, I admit. But, please, it never happened. Never happened. I'm getting married."

"Okay, Aunt Sally, I'll come over later to check on you."

"Okay, you've got somebody in your office. I get it. But, look, don't call me. Please. I have a life to get on with. Zygmunt, do not call! Don't write. Don't email. I don't want to see or hear from you again. Please try to understand. Please don't contact me in any way, shape, or –"

Sent: 14/06/2003 9:45 a.m.
To: hmarkson9077@gmail.com
From: zygadams@sympatico.ca
Subject: This u won't believe

Nomad, tried to get u on your cellphone, but all I get is the goddamn answering service that tells me you haven't subscribed.

Joan-e will put a contract out on me if she ever hears about this. That bitch Marianne from our box at the ballpark a couple of years ago cancelled out on me at the last minute, and who the hell else should Joan-e fix me up with last night at the last minute for the Mariachi Gala? It was Antoinette, the woman I told you about a couple of weeks ago.

Antoinette and I argued the whole goddamn night about everything. To keep in Joan-e's good books and against my will and better judgment, I saw Antoinette home to her apartment. Being the gentleman I am, as u well know, I went to give her a little good-night peck on the cheek just to be polite. Well, one thing led to another and the next thing I know we're are in the sack. That's a first for me. Nothing like that ever happened to me before. Never. I swear.

I knew she was engaged. She made that very clear at dinner. And that's why she phoned me this morning at my office. I was in a meeting with this tough security cop about my car being broken into yesterday. She said it was all a huge mistake and to forget the whole thing.

But I'm having no trouble remembering A's name like I did with Marianne from the ballpark. As a matter of fact, I can't get it out of my mind. The problem in a pea shell is she wants nothing to do with me. Could it be that my carefree, fun-loving reputation preceded me? There could be some other reason, of course. My compact stature, my overwhelming good looks, or malicious rumours spread about me as a womanizer, or lecher or whatever. Or by some remote chance it could be because she's getting married in three weeks.

Got any ideas for me?

Zyg.

P.S. By the way, on the weekend, I bought a townhouse up in the old Annex area on Admiral Crescent. I'll be moving in next month. I'll have a huge mortgage, but finally be a homeowner with a mortgage like everybody else. That feels good. When you decide to come back to Toronto to hunt for a new job, you're welcome to stay with me (rent-free, if you look after the garbage).

Sent from my BlackBerry.

A reply didn't come from Harvey until after the weekend:

Sent: 17/06/2003 9:45 a.m.
To: zygadams@sympatico.ca
From: hmarkson9077@gmail.com
Re: This u won't believe

I never know what time zone I'm in, so I don't use the answering service. Email or text is the best way to get me. I can pick it up on my BlackBerry whenever I'm free or awake.

As for my advice, if I came to you with that Antoinette Mairie story, you'd tell me to get a shrink immediately, wouldn't you, you dumb jerk? So here's my advice to you, my friend, if you really want it. **RUN. DO NOT WALK. RUN. RUN FOR THE NEAREST EXIT AS FAST AS YOU CAN.**

But I know you. A comment like that only brings out your competitive nature. You'll chase after her, betrothed or not. So forget I said anything. I don't want to feel I'm wasting my breath.

All I can do is simply beg you to come to your senses, knowing that's the last thing on earth you're likely to do. Unfortunately, I won't be around this time to help clean up the spilled blood, which in this case most likely will be yours. If I know you, the next thing I'll hear about is you under her apartment balcony professing your eternal love. I certainly don't remember you as some sort of professor of love.

Tu amigo,

Harvey.

Barcelona, España

P.S. Getting out of town might help. I'll be back in Bermuda, a week Thursday. Why not come down for a few days? I'm having trouble finding backgammon victims on the island.

Harvey was quite right, of course. Zyg didn't heed his advice, not for a second. In truth, the campaign for Antoinette in the summer of 2003 (Code Name: Campaign Sleepover) had begun three days earlier, the moment he'd hung up from the Aunt Sally call.

In spite of the assurances given over the phone with the security guard in attendance, Zyg didn't try to make further contact with Antoinette that day. She would have been fully prepared for such a foray, armed to the teeth with refusals. That he knew. And any email sent would end up in the junk mail or the deleted folder. Zyg's first move was to make no move. And with that, he felt the Sleepover campaign was off to a good start.

At lunch discussing a $22 million takeover of Craig Windows, The Pirate had to ask Zyg on three different occasions if he really wanted to work on the deal. In a lunch-hour squash game the next day, he lost all three matches – 15–3, 15–1, and 15–1. Usually, he got at least five points. He turned down two dinner invitations on the weekend. Watching the baseball game or the world dart championships in his apartment helped not one bit. One evening at about midnight he drove past Antoinette's apartment building as if proximity could ease the tension. It didn't. And he knew time wasn't on his side. With warlike campaigns, it seldom is.

The first skirmish you could hardly call a success. Assuming the law courts were closed and the voice mail wasn't on yet, he phoned Antoinette's office about 4:30 the following Monday.

"May I say who's calling?"

"It's just the tag board from her tennis club," Zyg replied in a high falsetto.

"Could I give Ms. Mairie a name in case she's busy and wants to call you back?"

"Regina."

"Is there a last name?"

"Saskatchewan," Zyg blurted, and hung up.

A very carelessly planned attack, he had to admit. Even if he'd gotten through to Antoinette, what good would that have done? She could have hung up at any point she felt like. Much more preparation went into his "second offensive" launched the following Thursday.

Picture a man, somewhat short in stature, in the late afternoon behind the wheel of his Porsche parked on the street across from Antoinette's apartment building. The man is dressed in a dark grey uniform with a luminescent green *speedyRwe©* emblazoned above the breast pocket of a windbreaker two sizes too large and a chauffeur's cap resting upon his ears and the top rims of his thick-lensed glasses. A woman in a blue Volvo drives into the garage entrance of the apartment building across the way. The uniformed driver glances at his watch, waits ten minutes, and gets out of the car with a crate and a sports bag in his hands. He approaches and enters the building. The man plunks down a delivery slip for the concierge, opens the crate door, and holding an index finger to his mouth, says in a very soft voice, "A surprise."

"Oh, Miss Mairie, there's a courier down here with a package for you. May I send him up…? Looks like another wedding gift…. I'll check…. From a Mrs. Joan Malone…. Okay, then…."

The *speedyRwe©* courier rides the elevator up to the apartment, and before he presses the buzzer, takes out of the crate a coffee-brown poodle puppy with eyelashes so long they look false.

Constrained by a brass chain, the apartment door opens no more than a couple of inches. A hand with a $2 coin in its grasp slides over the chain.

"Thanks, Courier," says a voice from behind the door. "Just leave the package on the floor, please, and I'll bring it in later."

"The package is alive, ma'am."

The door closes and then, unchained, opens again.

"For you, ma'am," the deep-voiced courier says, head down, his hand holding out the puppy.

The scene is set then. And here's what followed.

Antoinette took the dog in her arms and cuddled it. "Does he have a name?"

"He's one of the few dogs in the world that can say his own name," the courier said, his voice not quite as deep as before. "It's Woof-Woof. Got him through a friend of mine at the racetrack."

"Mr. Adams, you bastard!"

"Can we talk? Just for a minute, I mean?"

"Mr. Adams, why a clever man like you can't get my point is beyond me. I don't wish to talk to you. Or, for that matter, to Miss Saskatchewan supposedly from my tennis club, either. I'm to be married. Funny, you speak English well enough, and yet you seem completely incapable of grasping the simple notion of 'no.'" Antoinette hugged Woof-Woof. "Your friend here is adorable. Did Joan really send him? Of course not. She wouldn't have any part of this."

"He's a present from me to you. Everything's here in the sports bag – food, treats, leash, bed, dog bowls, doggie bags, everything."

"He's a lovely little creature. Maybe I could change his name to Zygmunt. My future husband would love hearing that every day," she said as she handed Woof-Woof back. "Obviously, that wouldn't work too well. Mr. Adams, may I ask you along with your adorable little friend, in the politest way possible, to leave?" She stroked Woof-Woof's coat again.

"But, Antoinette, listen to me for a minute, just for a minute."

"What?"

[An elevator pitch is often used by entrepreneurs to present in a quick manner the essential ideas to gain interest in funding for their enterprises. But elevator pitches are also used in many other situations. Personal uses include job interviewing, dating, and summarizing professional services. Accessed at http://en.wikipedia.org/wiki/Elevator_pitch.]

From his deal-doing days, Zyg was a pro at elevator pitches. Of course, he had prepared one for this occasion and had rehearsed it a dozen times and even one last time while waiting in the car. It was to include the suggestion of dinner somewhere out of town to discuss the compelling benefits of what would be referred to as "The Zyg Option." With the stage set, the elevator door open, so to speak, the rehearsed words refused to come forth. Instead …

"I want to … I want to profess my love."

Little Woof-Woof tilted his head as if dumbfounded. Antoinette seemed equally dumbfounded. "You want to profess your love, Mr. Adams? For whom? You? In love with somebody other than yourself, Mr. Adams? In the scheme of things, I think that's not bloody likely."

"It's true. I'm in love with you."

"Mr. Adams, quite frankly, I think you'd be one of the last people on the planet to know what it is to love another person. I suspect, Mr. Adams, you're one of those Bay Street gentlemen who has great difficulty distinguishing between love and lust. Divorce lawyers like me come across that problem quite commonly in our practice."

"I mean every word."

"You know what I think, Mr. Adams? I think that's a very careless use of language. Very careless. I'm already late for dinner. I have to go. Woof-Woof is a lovely, just lovely little guy." Antoinette petted the dog again. "But, of course, I can't accept him. So let me thank you. It was sweet of you to think I might enjoy his company. You're perceptive. That I have to admit. Thank you all the same and good night, Mr. Adams, and good night to you, too, little Woof-Woof."

"A careless usage of language, a careless use of language," said Zygmunt to himself as he and the dog exited the building, one of them with his tail between his legs.

Campaign Sleepover came to a sudden halt. In fact, the only one to get a sleepover out of the whole effort was Woof-Woof.

■ ■ ■

Since I was going to be out town visiting a cousin of mine in Chicago, Joan-e, who didn't know a thing about Zyg's recent "declaration," asked him to escort her to Antoinette's wedding. Long after the fact he told me he kind of liked the idea of going through the receiving line and whispering to her to keep in mind "The Zyg Option" as a fallback. Or presenting her with a gift certificate for a full set of the *Oxford English Dictionary* just to show he wasn't a poor loser. But he thought better of it.

On the Saturday night the wedding took place, shortly after nine o'clock, Zyg switched off the TV. Neither the baseball game nor the semifinals of the English Premier Dart League were capable of holding his attention. He got in his Porsche and drove to the Wild Goose, his old hangout. He hadn't been back there since exiling himself to Vancouver. He almost drove right by, not recognizing the addition on the roof of a giant goose outlined in yellow neon, its red beak blinking on and off, throbbing against the background of the night sky.

While outwardly the Wild Goose might have changed, its innards had been altered not one bit. The same old homey odours of stale alcohol and frying fat hovered in the air. The shabby brown leather banquette seats hadn't been refurbished nor had the dilapidated tables. The dark wood panelling and the yellow metal ceiling hadn't seen fresh paint, nor had the dull green walls with the same old photographs of geese, ducks, and quails migrating hither and thither. The television sets in each corner of the room just below the ceiling blinked away unheard over the loud chatter and piped-in music. One of the waiters seemed to recognize Zyg, greeted him with a big smile, and held out his hand. But then he merely mumbled, "Long time no see, buddy."

Zyg sat down at the end of the bar – in the old days always an excellent starting point and only on the rarest of evenings a place where he finished. He ordered a Stooby's India Pale and swung around on his stool to scan the room for "Gosling" regulars he knew. Zyg did recognize one of the waitresses who'd come home with him one night. Renewing that relationship meant waiting around until closing time and the long process of sharing her tips of the evening with the bartender and busboys. He was too tired for that. As he started on a second beer, a tall redhead he recognized came in and sat at a table by herself. Though she taught yoga, purportedly Tantric yoga, at a wellness centre down the road, she had remained elusive despite Zyg's extended efforts. Remembering her fondness for Prosecco, Zyg sent a bottle over with the bartender who arrived at her table at the same time as a tall, gangly fellow wearing a yellow basketball jacket with two red giraffes on the back. The only communication Zyg had with her was a kiss blown in his direction and a two-thumbs-up sign as he walked toward the door.

On the way home, his Porsche insisted, or so his email to Harvey said, on driving by Antoinette's old apartment building, the scene of the courier fiasco three weeks earlier. Neither the drive-by nor the expedition in search of a Gosling companion provided any relief. He simply couldn't get Antoinette out of his thoughts.

Scrolling through the *M*'s on his BlackBerry contact list a few nights later, he landed by sheer chance on Mademoiselle Mairie's name. After that anybody whose last name began with *M* prompted thoughts of her, even the name of Tyler McCrobie who, on Joan-e's recommendation, was to supply a special fertilizer for 85 Admiral Crescent's new flower beds.

Or here's another example. On an overnight business trip to Montreal two weeks after Antoinette's wedding, Zyg got through his meetings early and had an hour to kill before catching the plane home. At the gala Antoinette had mentioned how as a child she used to toboggan on "The Mountain" (as Montrealers call the high hill in the middle of their city). So he got a cab driver to take him up to The Lookout, an exercise that was somehow meant to bring him back to his senses and convince him he was no longer the young man who had fled to Canada two decades earlier, overcome by a woman's rejection. But the view of the city from The Lookout like the visit to the Wild Goose and the drive past the apartment where he had professed his love couldn't rid his mind of Antoinette, nor his body of the feelings of loss and regret, nor the hovering, aching sadness. It seemed nothing could heal that wound … except time. But he'd learned all too well twenty years before that time can be as slow as molasses.

∎ ∎ ∎

One day downtown Zyg was sure he spotted Antoinette entering one of the bank towers on Bay Street. The quiet frenzy returned instantly. Slowly, though, other factors intruded into his life and took up his attention. The Pirate had him working on the purchase of a large retail mall fifty miles north of Toronto. Another deal, the sale of Home Safe Home Security Systems, moved to the front burner the day before he took possession of his new townhouse. Zyg hadn't recovered completely from the outsized loss he'd taken when Save Your Time Software limped into bankruptcy. He needed to see those deals consummated. Still, one way or another, thoughts of Antoinette invaded in his mind and took their own sweet time leaving.

Why is it we can understand the movements of celestial bodies indiscernible in the night sky or of bodies so small as to be unobservable to the naked eye, yet not the movements of the heart? Why is it so difficult for us to grasp why we are loved if we are? Or why we aren't if we're not?

∎ ∎ ∎

One Saturday morning in September, the summer recently departed, Zyg dozed off on the couch, the only piece of furniture in his living room. Little Woof-Woof, who had a decided preference for sleeping next to a warm body, was stretched out beside him. Then the phone rang.

"Oh, Zygmunt, good morning," a voice said when he picked up the phone. "Hope I'm not disturbing you. It's Antoinette."

"Antoinette? My favourite service manager over at my Porsche dealer? How are you?"

"No, Antoinette Mairie, Joan's friend."

"Oh, that Antoinette."

"Yes, that Antoinette," she said with a slight laugh.

"You want your dog back?"

"No, I need some help."

"Are you sure you've got the right number?"

"Can I come over and talk?"

"I've been too busy to work on my language usage. But you're welcome all the same."

"I'm on my way into the city."

"You're serious?"

"Yes."

"I'm at 85 Admiral Crescent, three blocks north of the university."

"A client of mine lived on Admiral. I know the street."

Twenty minutes later, seated on one of the four kitchen chairs, the only horizontal surfaces on the main floor suitable for sitting other than the living room couch, Woof-Woof on her lap, Antoinette said, "I like your minimalist approach."

"I have a couple of more pieces coming next week."

"It's a lovely old house. Good bones. I like it."

"At the present rate I should have it fully furnished by the middle of the century," Zyg said as he poured Antoinette a cup of coffee.

"Furniture would make a world of difference." Antoinette was dressed in a dark grey pantsuit and was on the way to her office. That cheeky smile usually resident on her face was absent. Quite the opposite. She looked very tired.

"Haven't had a chance to get my dictionaries unpacked yet," Zyg said as he sat back down at the table.

"I was pretty tough on you, wasn't I? But, Zygmunt, I had to discourage you. Today, though, I'm not feeling quite so tough."

The weekend before, she explained, she and her new husband had invited friends over for dinner. Instead of offering cocktails, her husband brought out a bottle of champagne and announced his appointment as head of the Far East Division of the marketing consulting firm he worked for. After the guests left, he told her he'd put their condo on the market that day, since they'd be moving to Hong Kong.

"To say I wasn't hot about the idea," Antoinette said, "would be like saying Churchill wasn't crazy about Hitler invading Poland. What was I supposed to do? Give up my law practice and become dependent on him? I don't think so. I wouldn't want my financial well-being to depend on anybody other than me. I've seen what economic dependence can do to a woman's spirit. I'm good at what I do. I'm happy doing what I do. I help a lot of people. And China might be wonderful to visit, but it's last on my list of places I'd want to live, right up there with the South Pole and Burkina Faso. So, after the guests left, I told him so."

"More coffee?"

"Yes, thanks. I told him I wouldn't move to Hong Kong. He got furious. *Whew!* I knew he had a tough side from his days in the U.S. Marines, but I'd never seen him so angry. The last thing I was going to do was stand face to face with somebody trained in unarmed combat and that angry. I mean, with his training I had no idea whether he wanted to throw a 'monkey elbow' into my solar plexus and knock the wind out of me or drive my nose bones into my brain. I was frightened and ran into the bathroom and locked the door."

"That's wild. What did he do?"

"He started pounding on the bathroom door. If I hadn't left my cell-phone in my dressing gown in the bathroom by mistake, I don't know what would have happened. He only stopped when I told him I'd called 911. No cellphone and I might have been wearing quite a different face today."

Woof-Woof got down from her lap, took a drink of water from his bowl, and retired to the coolness of the kitchen floor.

"Sounds like a nightmare," Zyg said.

"My husband didn't stick around. He left before the police got there. I've no idea where he went. I heard him take his car keys from the bedroom. I didn't come out of the bathroom until I heard the police knocking on the door. I told them he'd gone out for a walk to cool off and everything would be okay. I put the chain back on the front door and stayed up all night. Couldn't sleep a wink. I asked the concierge to let me know if he returned. He didn't. In the morning, the concierge helped me load my suitcases and I drove out to my aunt's in my wreck of a car that really shouldn't even be on the highway."

"Can't you fix it?"

"The car?"

"No, your marriage."

"I took a long time – three years minimum – figuring out whether this was the right guy for me. I didn't want to go through the parting of ways I went through with my first so-called love back in Montreal. That was too painful." She sipped her coffee. "How stupid, stupid of me. Me of all people. If I can't spot a potential abuser when I see one – I hear about them every day in my business – who the hell can?"

"Why not move in here for a while. I'm looking for someone to head up the decorating committee?"

"No. Ah, that's very kind of you. I can't do that. I need to get my life back in order. I can stay with my aunt and uncle in Oakville until I buy a condo. But I need to sell a bunch of stocks. That's why I wanted to talk to you. Can you find me a broker, somebody I can trust? There must be somebody."

"Not easily. It's getting harder and harder to find anyone on The Street willing to take time off – too busy with their orgies. Should be somebody, though. Won't be easy. Hold on! I've got just the guy. Smart and knows the market inside and out. And honest as the day is long …"

5
A Labour of Love

Late September 2003

"That was a mistake. A huge mistake. You haven't a clue how to play tennis," Antoinette said. The sun had just about called it a day and the court lights had taken over.

She and Zyg walked up the cobblestone path toward the clubhouse of the Elm Tree Tennis Club (known simply as "The Elm Tree," though disease had killed off every last elm years before). It was one of those unexpectedly warm fall evenings. A sweet smell hung in the air thanks to the remaining maples and oaks, their leaves starting to turn. Wispy pink-tinted clouds scattered themselves across the sky.

"You say. But who won? Six-two. Six-two."

"That's beside the point. All you do is play squash on a tennis court. All those stupid cut shots and drop shots. You didn't hit the ball squarely once. Not once. Well, guess what, that's the first and last time you and I will be on a tennis court together. You can count on that."

"I thought it was pretty even. Maybe I'm a step faster."

"A step faster. You ran around like a maimed rhinoceros. Thank God we were on a back court. At least nobody saw us. It'll take me weeks to get my swing back. That wasn't fair, Zygmunt. You said you could play tennis."

"Excuse me? I've learned to choose my words carefully. What I said was I knew my way around with a racquet."

"Well, once again you overstated your case. I think you should stick to squash, or maybe Ping-Pong." Antoinette's tone softened. "What would you like to drink? You don't deserve one, but my father taught me to always be polite to guests."

"Why don't you shower and change and come back to my place for takeout? After a workout like that, we deserve something special. I've got a fabulous new Californian Zinfandel to try."

"I can't be late. I told my aunt I'd be home after tennis. She'll worry. I feel like a teenager on curfew. I don't know how I got myself into this jackpot. Okay. You go ahead. I'll change and come over."

A couple of hours later the phone rang.

"Who in hell would phone on a Friday at this hour? Mind if I take it? Might be Harvey Markson from Bermuda. Been trying to get him all week."

Zyg let the phone ring a third time, then picked it up and said in a deep, modulated voice, "You have reached 968-7174, Zyg Adams's residence. If you would like to leave a message, please do so after the beep." Zyg made a beep sound.

"Oh, Zygmunt, good evening. It's Edgar Parsons down at IED Securities. We haven't spoken for some time. I wonder if you would be kind enough to give me a call at home this weekend. There's an important matter I'd like to discuss with you. Thanks. My number is –"

"Edgar, it's Zyg. How've you been? You're right. We haven't talked for some time."

"Zygmunt? Oh, Zygmunt, is that you? I thought I was getting your voice mail."

"I haven't gotten around to setting it up yet. Just wanted to make sure it wasn't a crank call. You never know these days."

"Yes, well, sorry to ring you so late. Frankly, I didn't expect you home on a Friday night."

"No problem, Edgar. I'm in for the evening."

Perhaps it was the Pommard. Edgar's voice boomed into the bedroom like that of a game-show announcer. Zyg held the phone away from his ear. Edgar cleared his throat.

"In confidence, Zygmunt, we've a bit of a challenge on our hands down here, you might or might not have heard. Big Bobby's a nice fellow, a wonderful bloke actually. But we've come to realize, however, the job's a bit much for him, you know. So he'll be leaving us shortly. What we need, we now realize, is strong all-round leadership, not just a hotshot of a salesman. We need a person who understands this business in all its aspects, not just sales. We all agree you have those qualifications and would make an excellent CEO. We think you'd be someone who could move our little company forward."

"Who's we?"

"Essentially Skly, Don-Phil, and me, of course."

"What about Chable?"

"Sherwin? Not to worry. He's hardly involved these days. The only thing he cares about these days is his golf handicap and his bad knee." Edgar gave another quick cough. "Of course, he wants to see change around here every bit as much as the rest of us. In his own way, perhaps even more."

"You guys must be really desperate. I'm sure you wouldn't get much of a reference from Eldred Donnis after I told him what he could do with his Sheardon-Cassidy."

"Oh, we heard all about that. Yes, of course. We also know how Eldred's thinking can be a little short-term at times. But you would be the boss here, not Sherwin. And obviously not Eldred." Edgar gave another nervous little cough. "Look, I've probably interrupted something."

"No, not really," Zyg said as he reached over and gently pulled Antoinette back down to the bed.

"Look, why don't I arrange a suite for us at the King Eddy Monday afternoon?" Edgar suggested. "We could talk at the hotel, you know, in confidence. All this is in total confidence, right?"

"Yes, of course."

"My secretary will phone you Monday morning with the room number. Come down and chat with us, that's all. You wouldn't be committing yourself to anything in any way. Not in any way whatsoever."

"One question, Edgar. Do you guys truly believe a company your size can survive against the big banks? We all know there's nothing they'd love more than to swallow all you small fish for breakfast."

"They're much bigger than we are, that's true. But you know, Zyg, how awfully clumsy and slow they can be at times. That can be said of us, too. But there's definitely a market for smaller independent firms like ours. Clients feel there's more humanity, much more humanity, in the way we treat them. They don't feel they're on some sort of assembly line."

"And with Chable? I mean, for me it would be out of the kettle and into the fire. You got to give Bobby credit. I don't know how the hell he put up with Sherwin. Is Bobby okay?"

"Moving on is never easy for anybody," Edgar said, then paused. "Don't worry. You'll have complete control. Otherwise no deal. We understand that. Don-Phil and Skly understand that. Chable would understand that. He'd have to."

"After that six-year nightmare with Donnis, I don't see a helluva lot of difference between the two companies. Donnis was bad enough. Now that Sherwin's got dough, I'll bet he's worse than ever." Zyg continued to balk, but his words began to sound more like a negotiating stance. Finally, he agreed to meet with the Crisis/Search Committee on Monday and the phone conversation ended.

"Hey, where do you think you're going?" he asked as he kissed Antoinette's naked shoulder.

"Back to my aunt's. Nobody in the world will believe I was out playing tennis till this hour." She swivelled and returned Zyg's kiss with a slow, unhurried kiss to his shoulder. She stared up at him for a moment and then off into space. Then she rolled to the far side of the bed and got up. "Sherwin Chable would be your chairman?"

"You know the guy?"

"A little. From court. He'd make Moammar Gadhafi look like Mother Teresa. I represented his wife. She was a lovely woman. Lot of dignity. He didn't want to give her a nickel, not a nickel, and he was the party walking out."

"Sounds like Sherwin."

"I think you had the right instinct in the first place. Taking IED on would be a huge mistake. Just like my inviting you to play tennis." She held her bra in one hand while the other hand wagged a finger at him. "And you should respect my opinion." Her face fell sad. "When it comes to errors in judgment, God knows, I'm the queen. The Queen of Blunders. I can't even keep a marriage going for three months."

"Hey-hey, Your Highness, take it easy on yourself. If people got things right all the time, the stock market would never go down." Zyg put one hand behind his head and stared up at the ceiling. "I'm happy doing deals. And you're probably right. Those guys must be desperate. And I'd have to be stark-raving nuts to want to run a place like IED. Absolutely stark-raving goddamn nuts."

"I quite agree, Mr. Adams, if you think there's a chance you could save a run-down bucket shop like that from self-destruction," Antoinette said as she snapped her bra into place and took her glasses from the bedside table. "Then again, a guy like you might like it in the saviour business. It can be quite challenging, they say."

■ ■ ■

"How's it going?" Zyg asked, the phone in one hand and checking his emails with the other.

"I'm way behind. I'm in court tomorrow against another one of your Bay Street beauties who doesn't care to pay up. And ... and I've got to find a place to live somewhere downtown. Getting into the city is a killer."

"How about 85 Admiral Crescent? We have an introductory offer on this week only. Free rent for the first five years."

"Thanks for getting Kopsin to look at my portfolio," Antoinette said, ignoring Zyg's offer. "The Combatant, that last husband of mine – the very last – followed the market like a private eye. I went along with whatever he and his broker buddy decided. No idea whether I made a nickel. That's how much faith I had in him."

"Kopsin thought you could sell just about everything if you need cash right away. If you don't, you should hold on to the oils for a while. He'll send someone over to your office tomorrow to sign you up as a client."

"You're a peach. I take back every mean thing I ever said to you."

"You still on for Friday night?"

"Sure. By the way, how'd your interview go with those deadbeats from IED?"

Zyg deleted a couple of emails. "Still mulling it over."

"Why in the world would you want to take on something like IED? Any place that had Chable in charge is bound to be overstocked in moral dwarfs. Like that wonderful bloke Big Bobby." Antoinette imitated Edgar Parsons, cough and all. "I'll bet he's an absolutely wonderful bloke. In fact, I'd also bet there aren't enough garbage trucks in town to haul away all the junk he's unloaded over the years."

"You know I like challenges. Fixing real-estate deals gone sour, rescuing broken-down brokerage houses, teaching mature women tennis – that's what I do for a living. I do challenges."

"So it's back to Bay Street Bingo for you, Mr. Adams." Antoinette began imitating Parsons's high-pitched voice again. "Under the *B*, Bre-X. Under the *N*, Nortel. Under the *G* ... Sir, we happen to have a few shares of the Great B.S. Company of Canada left. True, at the moment there's an oversupply of bullshit, especially with an election coming up."

"Very funny."

"Seriously, why are you doing this, Zyg?"

"I told them their business model had seen better days. They said to come up with a new one. That's the part that interests me. It's a chance to do something different. I'd get Kopsin as the investment brains. He'd design the clients' portfolios. We'd operate more like an advertising agency. He'd be the creative department. And the reps more like account executives than salesmen. They wouldn't have to blow their brains out trying to figure what the market's up to next."

"Well, that part's a good idea. Brains are in short supply on The Street as it is. They think everything Ottawa does is stupid. But not for a second do they question if what Bay Street does is good for anybody other than themselves. Never. Not for a second."

"What are you talking about?" Zyg asked.

"You have to be a moral dwarf to believe the only people on earth that count for anything are shareholders. Don't employees count? Or people in the local community? You really think you could get parasites like that to change the way they think?"

"Course not. Not on my own. I'm counting on assistance from a well-known industry critic, Mademoiselle Antoinette Mairie. I want to show her some people on The Street are motivated by things other than sex and money."

"My God, you're serious."

"Could turn out to be a labour of love."

"Ho-ho, you, Mr. Adams, involved in a labour of love? Not likely. A labour of lust – that I could see. But a labour of love? No way. Then again, to repeat myself, a guy like you might like it in the saviour business."

6

Saviour Inc.

For Winnipeg, Zyg's approach would mean its worst fears had come to life. There was nothing in this whole still-green world that Winnipeg hated more than Toronto telling them what to do. Now, with a new CEO in "The Grand Ballroom," head office would want to dictate to them account for account, client for client, stock for stock, word for word, exactly how to do their business.

The new CEO's memo talked about organizing IED, more like an advertising agency. And it mentioned getting out of selling new issues of stock (initial public offerings, IPOs in the obfuscating lingo of The Street) because that created conflicts of interest. In the past, selling IPOs had been an excellent source of revenue for the reps and for the firm but, unfortunately, they were seldom a good deal for clients (Pluman's Funeral Homes simply one good example). The memo also said that in the future all commissions, including those for the sale or purchase of bonds ("haircuts" in Street Talk), must be fully disclosed to the client.

That last point didn't go down well at all with Cross Bennett. For years he'd been admonishing the reps in his office for giving clients "trims" instead of "full-scale brush cuts" on bond trades. In fact, Cross was so insistent on this practice that several reps referred to him, when out of earshot, as "The Barber of Civil," or sometimes just as "The Civilian."

During his fifty-five years, Cross Bennett had uttered, no doubt, many a scatological word combination, the kind more commonly heard on construction sites, in army barracks, or in boardrooms of prestigious financial houses. Today, however, those phrases have become so commonplace that you hear them at dinner parties, lunch counters, and even from the lips of four-year-olds at breakfast. So, perhaps unconsciously, at least so he claimed later, Cross chose the vocabulary of a four-year-old to express his sentiments. As he read Zyg's memo, his complexion turned florid red, and to his empty office the words he uttered in a muffled shout were: "Yuck! Yuck! Yuck!"

What is it in our nature that makes us conclude so readily the inevitability of the most unfavourable outcome? How often have you seen what at first glance looked like a permanent intrusion of bleakness into your life turn out in the end to be quite the opposite? Take, for example, the funk Mr. Cliffy went into for three days when he missed out on a chance to buy Everyday Is Satyrday, a speedy chestnut-brown stallion, he felt sure would have raised the brand of his Noblesse Oblige stable. In the late fall a couple of years later, in a race for three-year-old non-winners, the only horse his entry beat was Weekend Fun, a daughter of Satyrday. Not until then did Mr. Cliffy realize that the great Satyrday, horse of the year in 1993, had passed on not one "lick" of his speed to his progeny and that he would have brought nothing but shame to the already questioned brand of Noblesse Oblige Farms.

Or when Roger Belknap snapped his ankle in a squash game at The Racquets, he bemoaned his lot to anybody who would listen as he hobbled around the club in a leg cast. As it turned out, his physiotherapist gently prompted Roger back to better-than-ever fitness, and after his recovery, he played the best squash of his life. Not only that, the therapist became his third wife, giving him years of happy married life right up until his death in a heli-skiing accident north of Whistler, British Columbia.

And to emphasize the point, take Richard Gregory Lamens. Dick went into a full-scale tantrum followed by a serious depression when he missed out on the purchase of a large block of shares of Bre-X Minerals Ltd. The company ended up in bankruptcy and so might have Dick.

Only time can sort out the consequences of what at first blush looks like a disaster.

At that point in time, though, you couldn't have convinced Cross, not in a month of yucky Sundays, that anything good would befall him thanks to The Ballroom's new occupant.

The expression "Yuck" might have just as easily been chosen by Chicky Glickerman, Zyg's first boss at Sutton. When he read in the "Goings-On" column of *The World of Finance* that Kopsin T. Shurtz, B.A. M.A., LL.B., C.F.A., C.I.M., was moving to IED Securities Inc. as its new chief investment officer. Instead, he used more mature language and simply said he was "mucho pissed off." From watching Zyg's success at Sutton, Chicky had come to appreciate Kopsin's talents and knew Zyg's paycheque would shrink without this (unacknowledged) source of "good ideas" to suggest to his investing clients.

At the other end of the emotional scale, Kopsin, the perpetual Stoic, was delighted to be moving on. Not for the increase in income – his portfolio had grown well into seven figures and he was no spender. A two-room apartment; subscriptions to the sports channels to help with his bets on hockey, football, and baseball (a break-even proposition at best); a new car every nine or ten years; the takeout or pre-prepared food he ate while watching the sports channels; and the various medications he took not covered by his health insurance plan – those were the only big expenses in his life with one exception: his widowed mother liked to travel the world and only first class.

What drove Kopsin from Sutton was the ever-growing burden of being the compliance officer. The final straw for him came when one of the regulator's auditors reprimanded him for a photo missing from the supporting ID data of a founder of the Central Canada Society for the Prevention of Cruelty to Animals, who sat on the board of seven charities and was an Officer of the Order of Canada, but at ninety-two, still a possible undercover agent for Iran and its president, Mahmoud Ahmadinejad.

Kopsin couldn't keep up with both the capital markets and the unending demands of the regulators. He didn't have the time to protect everybody. It was a big enough job – in the name of compliance – to protect the security regulators and politicians from public criticism, and Cliffy Sutton and his staff from lawsuits, let alone the people who really needed the protection, Sutton's clients.

As chief investment officer of IED Securities, Kopsin could spend his entire day with the markets, the one true love of his life. But in time that would change. Time can change everything and often does.

Sent: 10/14/ 2003 9:45 p.m.
To: hmarkson2077@hotmail.com
From: zygadams@sympatico.ca
Subject: See Attachment

H, see the attached Word document. Too long to text.

Z

October 2003

Nomad, I never know where the hell u are anymore. How am I supposed to keep an eye on u? One minute you're in Cape Town, the next in Prague. You'll make a great travel agent if the QRS Bank ever gives u the shoe.

I know I should have admitted this to u earlier, but I didn't quite know how to. I've been seeing Antoinette. It's a very long story. Her new husband turned out to be quite a strange cat. He got a promotion to run Asia for his company and told A. she had to give up her law practice and move to Hong Kong with him. She refused. Gory details aside, that was the end of the marriage. It lasted less than three months.

After all that time with no hope, I was almost over her. At least I thought I was. There was a time my mind couldn't go five minutes without thinking about her. Now that problem is back worse than ever. Doesn't matter where I am. When the phone rings, the first thing I think of is: is it her? The first time I told her how I felt about her, you know what she said? Somebody like me couldn't possibly have a clue about love. Not one freaking clue, she said. What the hell? I'm a stock flogger and a deal-maker, not a shrink. But I know how I feel.

She works late most nights preparing her court cases. Her practice involves marriage split-ups mostly. She claims she's a specialist in un-love.

We do get together Friday nights, and she doesn't mind giving her body to me. That's a very lovely part of all this. She laughs and claims she inherited a touch of nymphomania from her mother. Just a touch, she insists. But she says she's put her heart in the penalty box for the next ten years for interference. She can't trust it anymore, she claims. On Saturday night, she usually babysits her aunt's dog so her aunt and uncle can play bridge at their church! Do u think God or somebody is trying to get back at me for my past?

And can u tell me why I would fall for someone with an IQ of five thousand and counting? How smart is that on my part? If I ever wanted to settle down, I had in mind a nice tender hausfrau, not some goddamn philosopher-queen advocate for justice. Maybe u should come up here and have a talk with her. On second thought, judging by her feelings toward her husband that was, I don't think she's into nomads.

On top of that, sometimes I think the *real reason* I took on IED was to prove to Antoinette that I'm not what she likes to calls a "typical Bay Streeter." She believes nobody can hold a job on The Street unless they believe the only two things that make the world go round are money and sex. I'm trying to show her that something else can go on, but I'm not quite sure what that something else is.

Be honest with me, Harv. Do u think I should try to get some help?

Z.

Zyg presented his fourteen-slide PowerPoint presentation in the IED boardroom for three different groups, the last time as a recorded webinar with Cross Bennett watching it on his desk monitor in Winnipeg. The show began like this:

Old Model: Car dealer = sales

NEW MODEL: AD AGENCY

= CREATIVITY + SERVICE

1

IED SECURITIES
STABILITY.
INTEGRITY.
COMPACTNESS.

"Gentlemen, if we change the business model from a sales organization to a service organization," Zyg said, "we'll become an entirely different kind of financial services provider. Different from everybody else on The Street. And if we aren't different – unique in some easy-to-tell way – IED won't survive, not for very long, anyway. That's the situation, as you all must be aware, that we face right at this moment. I know this is going to disturb some people. I get that. But let me be very clear why we're making these changes. Because if we don't, many of you will be out of a job, and the company will blow up or have to be sold. What we have to do is put Humpty Dumpty back together again, but in a new way. That's the object of all this – a new, 100-percent, customer-focused IED."

Zyg took a drink of water. "Our new strategy is very straightforward. We intend to kill our clients. Kill them with kindness. With efficiency. With satisfying their real needs. Not with idle promises we can't keep. No, with promises we can keep.

"We want our clients to feel good – so good – about doing business with us, with IED. We want them to feel so good about us that when their friends or lawyers or accountants go on the lookout for a new broker, our clients won't hesitate for a second to recommend us.

"In fact, they'll probably feel obliged to just the way you feel you have to tell people when you see a good movie or read a good book. You feel you're doing that person a real favour just letting them know about it."

Zyg clicked his remote and paused to give his audience time to read the new slide.

Kill our clients with

* Care & Concern

* Efficiency

* Promises Kept

2

IED Securities
Stability.
Integrity.
Compactness.

Next, he threw in an anecdote. "That's exactly how I became a big producer. It all started with one wealthy client. I'll call her Sally. Sally had a dozen brokers – one a husband – all of whom disappointed her in one way or another, especially the husband." Zyg paused, and a couple of people chuckled. "I made sure I never did. I was new in the business. I didn't know sweet anything. But whenever I told Sally I was going to do something, I made damn sure I did it. And then I told her I did it. And I always did it on time. And I always said thank you. Always said … thank you. I didn't know any other way to conduct business. Well, it wasn't long before Sally recommended me to her cousin, then to two good friends and even an ex-sister-in-law. I used the same strategy every time. I told them what I was going to do. Did it. And then told my new client exactly what I had done and when. And I always said thank you.

"To tell you the truth, all the cold calls I made in my early days – and I made plenty of them – brought in very few clients for all the effort and most of them turned out to be the wrong type. They really didn't need a broker. But over time referrals from Sally and from Sally's connections and from Sally's connections' connections began to flock in. And here's the best part: since birds of a feather flock together, they were the right type of client. People who wanted to manage their financial futures in one way or another.

"I'd like to take all the credit for the fact that I became a big producer. That's what I dreamed about the minute I stepped on The Street. But the truth is I had a secret weapon. Nobody's portfolio ever got into trouble. Sure, there were plenty of ups and downs. Things we bought too early and things we sold too late. But nobody ever got upset. Not one client left in 1991 when the market dropped five hundred points. Not one. Their investments never got into serious trouble. Why? Because I never made a move without consulting an expert, someone who made it his life to understand capital markets. And that expert has just agreed to join IED as our chief investment officer. He knows stocks and stock markets. And he never takes his eye off risk."

Zyg clicked to the next screen. So here's the change: you're not reps – account representatives – anymore. You're account executives. Your job is not to sell but to keep clients happy and content. We're not running a casino with you reps as the croupiers. We're running an investment service that breeds trust and deserves to be trusted."

"In the new model, you no longer have to pretend you understand markets – very few of us do. I know I'm not one of those few. And I suspect if you look at your own track records, you aren't very good at it, either, especially today with markets as complicated and competitive as they are. It's a professional market. Most of the trading is done by professionals and their computers. They know everything you and I know and most likely more. You will no longer need to be excited about things like the latest earnings report from XYZ Heavy Sweet Corn Oil or about its "EBITDA" cash flow. Can any of you tell me where the Canadian dollar will be a year from now? Where Dow Jones will be? What ten-year government bonds will pay?"

Again Zyg paused. "Besides, think about this. Do you really have time to be salesmen and service providers, and on top of those two jobs, both of them full-time, a market guru? No wonder you don't have enough time for your family. But with the new model, you won't have to spend half your life reading all those boring research reports, half of which you don't believe in the first place. You won't have to read five or six newspapers every day and click on ten or twenty different blogs every day before the market opens just to keep up in case a client asks you.

"Don't let me kid you, though. This won't be easy. There will be give-ups. We won't be handling IPOs anymore. New issues have that little extra vigorish that's so very attractive. But that's not the sort of incentive that's good for the client. I've seen too many portfolios stuck with IPOs that don't have a hope in hell of making any money anytime soon. Every client will have their own customized account. But the conversion to this new way will be far from easy – don't let me kid you – and it won't be quick and it won't be without cost to the company or without cost to you."

Nobody in the audience, in all three presentations, made a peep or even squirmed or snuck a peek at their BlackBerrys. Nobody excused himself or herself when after thirty minutes Zyg asked if anybody needed a bathroom break. Nor did that change for the next six slides that went into much greater detail.

"So your accounts will be handled in a completely different way. But here's the clincher. You'll have the best software on the street – best for handling transactions efficiently, best for meeting compliance requirements, and best, the absolute best, for handling relationships with your clients, keeping time-stamped notes, and preparing real financial plans. Five firms in the United States have had unbelievable success with this software, and we have the exclusive rights to it for Canada.

"Let me give you just one hint. You'll be able to customize each client's monthly statement so that he or she can understand it – easily. The information will suit the client, not the Back Office or the tax department. It won't show book values or the CUSIP number of each security unless that's what the client wants. It can be as simple as here's what you own, Mr. Client, here's what you paid for it, here's what it's worth today.

"My point is they will be statements customized to the level of understanding of the client involved whether he or she is an expert in statistics or wouldn't know the difference between volatility and Tylenol. That sort of thing will be a first for The Street, you have to admit. Of course, that will take work, lots of it, in the beginning. But you only have to customize the statements once with minor revisions as you learn more about your client or your client learns more.

"And this new software will save time and lower everybody's costs. So we'll charge fees – very reasonable fees – instead of commissions. You'll be earning money while you sleep or on the weekends, not just when you persuade someone to make a trade. And we'll constantly be at work to find ways to add value for those fees. All that will build your clients' trust in you and in us. And trust is the keystone to client satisfaction. So here's what you might see as the really best part."

Compensation

* Salary

* Profit Sharing

* Performance Shares

10

IED SECURITIES
STABILITY.
INTEGRITY.
COMPACTNESS.

"Every two weeks, rain or shine, a regular deposit will be made to your bank account. But at the end of the year there will be profit-sharing for everybody – frontline people, the Back Office, assistants, receptionist, everybody. Those who contribute more than the average will also get shares in the firm and the semi-annual dividends that go with those shares.

"What's the bottom line for all this? Less stress. After the start-up phase, less work. A better and more regular income. When you leave IED, we'll buy back your shares at the same price we sell them to employees at the time. And, of course, we'll buy your book of clients on a fair pre-established basis. No muss, no fuss.

"But what does this all mean to you? Plain and simple, it means you'll be an entrepreneur, in business for yourself. But also you'll be part of a team working together to make it better for everybody, including you and your clients."

Four more slides, including one on the arrangement of personnel, the org chart, followed. Again there was silence. No clapping. No murmuring. No squirming. It was as if nobody knew quite what to say or think. The presentation had lasted about fifty minutes. Zyg waited a few moments, then asked for questions.

Late that afternoon Cross Bennett emailed Zyg, lauding the idea of producing statements that clients could easily understand. Only one criticism was included: the plan wouldn't work. The changes would be a good idea, he wrote, if the main idea was to wipe out the Winnipeg office. The minute his reps got a whiff of these changes, they would be out the door to some other brokerage house down the street. No Winnipegger in his right mind was about to let anyone a thousand miles away tell him how to conduct business, let alone people from a town with a hockey team dedicated to perpetual mediocrity.

7
A Matter of Trust

"Hi, just checking in to see when our next game is," Zyg said, just having replied to three emails while on hold waiting for Antoinette.

"Never."

"Why' s that?"

"I don't play pretend tennis players."

"What if I try not to win?"

"Ho-ho! That's a good one, Mr. Adams. You? Try not to win? You change? Seen any spotless leopards lately? That's my new name for you – Spots."

"I want to know how your day went, Mademoiselle Antoinette."

"Well, Spots, I'll tell you, when your law partner goes on holiday, the phone never stops. I don't mind that. Leaves me less time to think about that wreckage of my last – my very last – marriage. Had a client today whose husband's as schizo as a traffic light. Changes his mind every two minutes. One minute he's says he's madly in love with her, the next he's out cheating his pants off. God, that's so male. I mean, how many men do you trust?"

"I trust Harvey. I trust Kopsin."

"That's excellent, Spots. Some three or four billion men in this world, and in your forty odd years, you've been able to uncover two you can trust. Two. A remarkable endorsement of the male species."

"And I trust my dentist."

"Didn't you tell me Harvey worked for some dentist? Kelpner, a Dr. Leon Kelpner, or something like that? Didn't you tell me that if that guy hadn't cheated somebody by the cocktail hour, he felt he hadn't done an honest day's work? Sounds like an upright individual to me. Just don't get gingivitis."

"Well, I trust most people. I trust my doctor."

"You nuts? Don't get me on that. They're the worst. After cancer and heart problems, you know who's the next biggest killer? Doctors and hospitals. And most hospitals don't even bother to track their mistakes. Wonderful. And when my poor sweet cousin ended up in hospital with a ruptured appendix, I had to put posters in his room instructing all staff to wash their hands before touching anything in the room, including my cousin.

"Hospitals today are nothing but iatrogenic inns. I mean, the last place you want to go if you're sick is to a hospital. Unless you want to get sicker. You can't get any sleep. They're always building a new wing or installing some machine in the room above you. My advice? Don't go to a hospital unless you're at death's door and you want someone to open it for you. And never, never, go to a hospital without an advocate of some kind. Never."

"Well, I suppose you can trust lawyers then." There was a long silence. "Are you multi-tasking or something?"

"Spots, about some things you're so naive," Antoinette said. "Hey, how did the Bingo go today? Anybody win a teddy bear? Under the *B* Bre-X. Under the *N* Nortel. Under the *I* –"

"I told you the only reason I'm down here working my heart out is to restore your faith in The Street."

"Well, you guys never play by the rules."

"What rules?"

"That's my point. You don't have any."

"I put in some today."

"Oh, forgive me, Zyg. Forgive me. Forgive me. I'm so inside myself these days. Wasn't this the day to make your big presentation? How'd it go? I'm sorry. That's terrible. Would I like your new rules?"

"One day, when you're a little older, I'll explain them to you."

"Well, more importantly, what did the IED folk think?"

"With those guys you never know. No standing ovations, mind you. They asked tons of questions, good questions, though. Everybody sounded okay with it. Everybody except that Neanderthal out in Winnipeg."

"What's his problem?"

"He said my business plan wouldn't work."

"You wouldn't let a little flaw like that stop you, would you? Just because something's not going to work, I can't imagine that stopping you, not for a second."

"People hate change. That guy is the worst of them all. I went through the same thing over at Sheardon-Cassidy. I just keep telling myself that things take time. But I don't know whether you noticed or not, patience isn't my strong suit."

"Well, except with me, you don't do patience well, not well at all."

"You can say that again in clubs."

2004

In business you never really know how things can fall apart at any moment. But after the first year or so, as far as Zyg could tell, IED Securities seemed to be coming around.

New accounts had begun to trickle in to the Toronto office, and the number of clients switching out to other firms had slowed to a similar trickle-like pace. True, some took their "play" money away and put it with competitors like Federal Wealth or Sutton. And clients who considered themselves expert stock pickers, like little Mary Margaret Murray, switched over to discount brokers. But most knew, especially after the beating they'd taken over the previous three years, that they needed help. If not help, at the very least they needed somebody to blame ("that jerk, my broker, told me 'don't sell' and a week later the sucker took a nosedive to twelve bucks"). Only two reps left IED: one for health reasons; the other confessed he couldn't live without the action of making trades all day long.

Zyg had gotten rid of much if not all of the shabbiness that hovered throughout the offices of the fourth floor of 370 Bay. The burnt-out bulbs in the reception area's chandelier were replaced two days after Zyg arrived on the job. One weekend the Back Office was painted from head to toe, and the next, new carpet was laid there and in the reception area and the embroidered rendering of the Great Wall of China was taken down. Many other small changes were made to the point that one rep, back from vacation two weeks later, thought he had entered the wrong office.

Nadia Whitall was stolen back by Zyg – the ace he'd brought to Sheardon but who had gone to work for Porter+Crampton, the people who turned the customer-service rating for Newfoundland Insurance from C to A- within a year. At lunch hour, Tuesdays and Thursdays for the first two months, members of IED met in groups of six with Nadia. People talked openly – in a way they would never have dared to before – about how best to handle the "mistakes, concerns, and situations" they had encountered the previous week. Even the Back Office, which had never participated in anything like a service-improvement program, began to treat the account execs (formerly reps) as clients instead of nuisances. Not quite equal to the parting of the Red Sea, but close.

On the other hand, some account execs didn't take to the scheme quickly and often came up with excuses that they were "under" something: under the weather, under family pressure, under doctor's orders, under an obligation to attend a distant cousin's funeral. Slowly, though, and not without a good deal of cajoling, the general morale at IED picked up, especially when the market started to climb out of the doldrums. Early on, Kopsin made some very good calls and positive results began to show up in clients' accounts. Slowly, in dribs and drabs, good humour returned to the halls and desks of IED Securities.

A rising market lifts all spirits.

When not in meetings, Zyg kept an open-door policy, so almost everybody in the secured executive area wandered in and out of his office all day long. And for at least an hour a day he'd wander around the fourth floor, talking to a secretary or an account exec, to an IT person or a research analyst or a Back Office administrator.

Toddy Landau, one of the triumvirate of big producers (known formerly as the Academicians) whom Zyg had persuaded to join Sheardon-Cassidy, called him and asked for an early-morning game of squash. Zyg knew something was up. Toddy could spot him a dozen points in a game and still win 15–13 without breaking a sweat.

"Well, I'll say one thing for your game, Zyg. You've left room for improvement," Toddy said as they sat down at a table in The Racquets snack bar, Zyg puffing like a train ascending an Andean mountain pass. "But I'd still give you an A for effort. Maybe, to be honest, you should find another sport."

"I've been looking. Maybe sumo wrestling. Maybe kite boarding."

Toddy pulled his chair a little closer to the table. "A couple of my clients mentioned how happy their friends were with the way you guys are doing business. They don't feel all that pressure to trade. And their accounts are doing well, or so they claim. Since Eldred sold us out to Federal Wealth, that same old feeling has returned, you know, of just being a little cog in some big bank's wheel of profit. We came over to Sheardon with you in the first place to get away from all that. We might just as well have stayed put."

"I was playing better squash in those days."

"Here's what I wanted to talk to you about. My son wants to get into the business. I don't want him working at Federal. I want him to be a true professional. You know, clients first, really first. That's how I built my book. Not just going through the motions and sending birthday cards."

"Well, we're trying to do it differently. Not easy. Not in the beginning. We have a lot to learn. And learning doesn't appeal to everybody. One of our guys dropped out because he missed the action. The guys know they're doing a much better job for their clients, but some complain they miss that thrill of trying to swing for four-baggers."

"Sure. But how about the excitement on the other side when the market tanks and you've got all that nursing and explaining to do?"

"That's a wall we haven't hit yet. We think we have clients prepared. You and I have been around long enough to know you never know."

"You know something else? I don't understand the markets anymore.

Maybe I never did. But with globalization and the computer and those 'algo' traders, you can't tell what's going on anymore. Or who to listen to."

Zyg looked at his watch. "If your son's looking for a job, Toddy, tell him to give me a call. I'm not sure we're ready to hire anybody yet. But let me think about it. And I'd be happy to talk to him."

"Well, my idea was that I would come over to IED first and then my son would join me when he gets out of school in the spring."

"Are you saying that the great Toddy Landau, the star member of The Academy, wants to come and work at IED? Are you kidding me?"

■ ■ ■

Other kinds of conversation took place.

"What do you mean you want to secede?" Cross Bennett's lawyer and stepfather asked him over the phone.

"I can't stand the thought of spending the rest of my days listening to those nutcrackers in Toronto telling me what to do. When they started all this new stuff, they didn't bother us with it. But now it's starting to pay off for them. They've added a whole bunch of new clients. And one of the big hitters on The Street came over to them from Federal. And Toronto's starting – again! – to think they're invincible. They want us to do it their way, turning us into stupid 'account executives' instead of real brokers. And they talk about this new guy who replaced Big Bobby as the chief equity strategist like he's smarter than Warren Buffett and George Soros rolled into one. I'll bet he is – until the next crash. You're my lawyer. You've got to find a way to get me out of this nightmare before they blow us up. This is a tragedy in the making, no question."

"Well, Cross, why don't you ask them how much they want for their Winnipeg operation? Have you got that kind of dough sitting around?"

"You know I don't, Daddy Fred. But get this. The great new chief investment officer was a compliance officer in his last place. What does a compliance officer know about anything? That's how you get to be a compliance officer, because you don't know anything about anything. And the new CEO those numbnuts just hired. This guy Adams. He's a sex fiend. An old school buddy of mine, Chicky Glickerman, who worked with Adams told me Adams joined a mixed book club for the sole reason of finding bed companions. All went well until a couple of the ladies began to compare notes. They threw him out on his ass. I mean, is that that the kind of guy you want heading up a prestigious firm like IED? Can you imagine having a sex maniac for a CEO? I mean, does that help to give our brand an aura of reliability and trustworthiness? I mean, Jee-sus Kee-riced! What were they thinking? A sex maniac, for Chrissake."

"For an organization like yours where, as far as I can tell, clients get diddled daily, I'd have thought that would be a *sine qua non* qualification," said the stepfather.

"That's not funny, Daddy Fred. Can't we sue them for breach of contract or something? I didn't join this outfit to be some sort of gopher for clients. I know how to manage portfolios. I didn't sit in on all those economics courses for nothing. I don't need Toronto to tell me how. If you don't want the case, maybe I should talk to somebody else."

"You can, but I don't think it'll help. Even if we were successful, it would cost you a ton of money and take two years to get to court – with luck."

"Well, could you look into it a little more?"

"Another thing. Getting the case together would take up a lot of your time. You'd have to spend your weekends at the office. What would that do to your golf game?"

"Okay. I hear you, Daddy Fred. Forget I even called."

Then Cross, as had Sherman Chable, hurled the phone receiver down and with such force that his executive assistant ran in to find out if something other than Wilfred Cross Bennett himself had blown up.

■ ■ ■

"You're really something, Mr. Adams, I must say. You really know how to work your way into a person's life, don't you? I'm surprised you haven't pitched a tent in my new condo. Your electric toothbrush and your shaving stuff take up a whole shelf in my medicine cabinet. I keep telling you all we have going is a series of one-night stands. But you want to turn it into a serious relationship. And that's exactly – the very thing – I'm trying to avoid. And so where do I find myself? Here with you." Antoinette threw her hands above her shoulders. "In a fabulous restaurant. I can even see the trees and the snow in Central Park. And I'm dining on the best lobster I've ever tasted in my life. And ... and I've only known you for a few months. And what's more, with my new life strategy, I'm not supposed to get to know you in the first place."

It had been no small task to get Antoinette out of Toronto, even for just a night. Persuading her took more than a month. She liked working weekends: "The phones don't ring and I can get things done, including my hair."

They had flown to New York that Saturday morning in time to drop their bags off at the New York Athletic Club (which had reciprocal privileges with The Racquets), grab a quick lunch, catch a matinee performance of *Cat on a Hot Tin Roof* on Forty-third Street, spend a couple of hours wandering in the Museum of Modern Art, walk from there over to the Asiate on Sixtieth for dinner with plans to catch a set later at the jazz club Birdland. A day designed for the pleasure of one Antoinette Josephine Mairie, the strained look on her face seeming just to enhance her appearance. She was wearing black slacks and a high-collared white jacket with buttons of interlaced gold strands running down from the lapels and around the cuffs.

"How about some dessert?" Zyg suggested. "Look at this. Mango pistachio gateau. What could be better than that, Antoinette?"

"You know I'm not big on sweets, especially cake," she snapped, as if returning from other thoughts.

"How about a liqueur then? A little Rémy Martin or something?"

"That'd be nice."

"Two of your best Rémy Martin," Zyg said to the waiter, then turned back to Antoinette. "Well, you told me you adore theatre, you adore New York, you adore art."

"I do. And so what do you do? You outright seduce me. My favourite gallery. One of my favourites plays. That scene where Big Daddy goes on about mendacity – that's real theatre. Williams must have been a broker at some point."

"Well, why did you agree to come down?"

"One good reason might be I'm human. I mean, how could I resist?

You salesmen know how to attack a person's weak spots. That's what selling is all about, isn't it? Break down their defences and you win."

"I just thought you needed a break really badly. You're working too hard. I'm not trying to sell you anything."

"I know, I know. You're so kind to me. Sometimes I get this wild idea – I admit it's wild – you're trying to sell me on love. And I'm sorry, but I'm not in the market for the stuff these days." Antoinette took his hand in hers. "That was cruel of me. I can be so glib at times. But my problem right now is I'm not big on getting involved at the moment. At this point I'm not sure I'd know love if it was standing on its head right in front of my face. In fact, I'm not sure anybody knows what that kind of love looks like anymore. People throw the word around as casually as a wet dishrag. The modern idea of love between two adults is so out of date. It's really an idea handed down from the troubadours and the knights in the 1100s."

"In the 1100s? That must be somewhere up around Ninety-first or Ninety-second Street."

Antoinette smiled a tired, lazy-lidded smile.

"You know what your problem is, Antoinette? You're as bad as Harvey. You think too much."

"You're right. But what you fail to realize is that when you strike out as badly as I did, you start to ask yourself a few questions. I thought I was in love with the Combatant, but I couldn't have been. Love doesn't just evaporate like that." She snapped her fingers. "Sure, he has a rage problem. But shouldn't I have tried to get him some help? I didn't. I didn't lift a finger. I just fled. In my mind he died that night. I mean, mentally I moved him into another world. He stopped existing in my mind. Where was my concern for him? Where was the caring? Nowhere. That's where. And what that tells me is I'm a loner just like my father. Nothing's more important to me than my independence. That has to be the absolute antithesis of love. Sometimes I feel I'm an isolated pocket of consciousness strolling around the planet unattached, unconnected to, or with, anything. It's like my mind has been put into solitary confinement for life. Not one link to the outside world. No Internet access. No email address. Not even a cellphone."

"Hey, we're down here to enjoy the city. That was the deal, right? We're supposed to forget about everything at home. We didn't come down here to analyze life. That we can do any day of the week back in Toronto."

The arrival of the snifters of cognac introduced a pause, but that's all. Antoinette wouldn't stop. "You're right. This isn't the place. But I don't want to mislead you. That wouldn't be right, either. Don't forget I'm in the un-love business. I deal in it every day. I sure as hell know what fake love looks like, believe me. If most of my clients had really been in love – had they got their hands on the genuine article – they wouldn't be clients. Most of them talk about their experience as if it was one huge con job. And now they want revenge or they want out as quickly and as painlessly as possible."

"Your clients aren't a fair sample. You're like a reporter on the crime beat. You get a warped perspective."

"Okay, but how does someone know they're in love? All they're really doing is reporting on their neurochemistry. They've got an excess of dopamine or oxytocin or serotonin in their head and they have to call it something, so they haul out the first word that comes to mind – love. Often as not, it's just plain old lust. Many of my clients don't seem to have figured out there's a difference. And you know who's worse?"

"The folks from Bay Street, right?"

"No, the very people who should know better. The psycho crowd. The psychologists and neuroscientists. They're the new plague. Half the time they can't distinguish between love and lust. But if there is no difference, people would say, 'Hey, honey, I'm feeling horny, let's get married.' Lust has a long history in the love business as an out-and-out imposter."

"Can I make one comment and then can we drop the subject? Before a guy tells some woman he loves her is he supposed to get out a dictionary and figure out which of the ten dozen meanings he has in mind?"

"No, of course not. But it has to be more than just uttering words. Nobody tries to demonstrate their love anymore. Anyone working with children in Uganda for five years just to prove their love to somebody?"

Zygmunt caught the waiter's eye, held a palm up, and slid the fingers of his other hand across it.

Once out on the street, Antoinette linked her arm through Zyg's. Anybody walking by would think the two were a happily married couple. But once across the intersection, she started up again, as if rehearsing a court pleading for the next day.

"But most relationships don't work out that way," Zyg interjected. "You're turned off on the world. I'm trying to help you regain a little faith."

"I guess I'm just tired, Reverend. Been up since 4:30 this morning. I've run out of steam. Mind if we skip Birdland?"

When they got up to their hotel room, they both fell asleep in their clothes, the bedside lights still on, and woke up the next morning with just enough time to catch their plane at JFK.

Antoinette had driven them to Pearson in her Volvo. That way, on their return, she could drive on to dinner with her aunt and uncle who she hadn't seen since she'd moved into her new condo. Zyg took a limo into the city, which gave him a quiet moment to reflect.

"What the hell's going on here?" he asked himself, all that buried anger coming to the surface. For him, it was like cold-calling in the old days, with one bad call after another. ("Nothing but a bunch of flaming thugs, you lot.") He had undertaken to resurrect IED, so you couldn't say he didn't like a challenge. But not one with odds that looked at that moment to be in the neighbourhood of a thousand to one against. That wasn't a challenge. That wasn't risk-taking. That was bungee jumping with a worn-out cord. "No thanks," he told himself.

As far as his relationship with Antoinette was concerned, right then and there in the limo, the Reverend Adams (aka Spots) decided to call it a day, though the sun was only halfway through its day's journey.

8

Ménage à Trois

February 2004

With Harvey gone, it became impossible to find squash opponents of a similar (low) calibre around The Racquets. To keep in shape, Zyg scheduled workouts with a personal trainer. And, at her suggestion, he alternated workouts with early-morning yoga classes (also walking up the four flights of stairs to his office at 370 rather than taking the elevator). At his first yoga class, while in the downward dog posture, he noticed on the next mat two white low-cut socks emblazoned with Nike swooshes that gave way to an unfamiliar pair of finely sculptured, unending legs. As he meditated, Zyg said to himself: "Now there might be a couple of members willing to take me on."

After class, Zyg commented to the owner of those legs on how adept she was at the poses. The compliment didn't stop her from thumbing away on her BlackBerry. Despite the significant discrepancy in height of the two practitioners, one thing led to another, and then to another, and eventually, Zyg's Admiral Crescent townhouse had a frequent overnight guest.

She was the sales manager of Allied-Faskin Pharmaceuticals and Medical Devices. She was a hard worker. No matter how hard she had worked at her daily drug dealings, though, she seemed to enjoy making dinner for IED's CEO or accompanying him to Thrace's or some other restaurant close by. Lizzy-Anne (her name was Elizabeth-Anne, never used by Zyg) was from a small town in the Ottawa Valley, an area, according to Harvey, where the best-looking women in Canada came from. No matter what time she arrived at Admiral Crescent, she always offered to take Woof-Woof for a walk, and slipped over at lunchtime from her office when the dog walker had an exam or couldn't make it for some other reason.

Admiral Crescent became a ménage à trois, Zyg and Woof-Woof making a majority of males in the master bed.

Sent: 15/10/2004 3:43 p.m.
From: hmarkson9077@gmail.com
To: zygadams@sympatico.ca
Subject: Email Received in Error

Sirs, I received an email yesterday from a Mr. Zygmunt Adams with the following warning: "Confidentiality Warning: This message and any attachments are intended only for the use of the intended recipient(s), are confidential, and may be privileged. If you are not the intended recipient, you are hereby notified that any review, retransmission, conversion to hard copy, copying, circulation, or other use of this message and any attachments is strictly prohibited. If you are not the intended recipient, please notify the sender immediately by return email and delete this message and any attachments from your system. Thank you."

May I point out that although I am familiar with a Mr. Z.A. of Toronto, there must be some mistake in that this gentleman claimed he was thinking of settling down with his new roommate(s).

It could not be the Z.A. I know. While I am known for an active imagination, it is not nearly powerful enough to imagine the Mr. Z.A. I know ceasing to climb into the bed with this or that female whether of short acquaintance or not. Such a monogamous role would never suit Z.A. who, in my opinion, is no more likely to settle down in our lifetime than the West Antarctic Ice Sheet. In fact, the latter is the more likely of the two.

However, the Z.A. I know would find India intriguing. There are many beautiful women here. Many. Many. And are they beautiful! If by chance we're talking about the same Z.A., tell him to forget the Ottawa Valley. Think the Indus Valley.

H. Markson
Hyderabad, Andhra Pradesh

Antoinette, later on, dismissed this interlude in Zyg's life as the "Big Pharma Period."

The only source of worry during those days for Zyg was IED and the constant flow of problems that accompanied change. Converting salespeople to service people was no easy task. For one thing, it was no easy task to teach seasoned reps (officially now called "account execs") to search for ways to help clients rather than trying to unearth trades.

Cross Bennett was still calling his reps "reps." "You want me to tell our guys to talk someone out of a sale? But that's all they know to do. How to get a client to buy something he doesn't want or to get him to sell something he wants to hold on to. That's what we train them to do, for Chrissake, Zyg. Otherwise, they're just order takers. You know the business as well as anybody. This all sounds like another one of those loser schemes you bright guys in Toronto dream up every time the market goes into the crapper."

"Well, Cross, how profitable is it to lose half you clients every time the market does that? Think how much time and effort and money it takes to replace the clients you lose. Selling people on things they don't want doesn't build trust. But keeping a person out of trouble does. Finding solutions to their problem does. Doing what you said you'd do does. Without trust you don't have clients. You're just running a drive-through with an outdated menu."

"Well, you come out here and tell that to the kid we just stole away from Federal. You tell him to forget all about commissions."

"That's not what I'm talking about. What I'm talking about is that neither that kid nor any of his clients has enough knowledge or skill to make a decent decision about whether to buy or sell the shares of Bombardier or RIM. But Kopsin does. Kopsin does because he eats and sleeps stocks thirty-six hours a day. And he's been doing that for twenty-eight years – or something like that – very successfully. He's got more information crammed into his snivelling head then a ten-storey reference library. The job of a frontline person like your new kid is to solve the client's problems that go along with investing – making sure a client isn't taking more risk than he or she can stomach, encouraging them to save, showing them how to reduce taxes, helping them get their affairs straight with the right powers of attorney and get their estates in order with an up-to-date will. But only full-time professional money managers like Kopsin should be figuring out what's appropriate for a client's portfolio. Even you, Cross, and you're a good stock picker I've heard, could save yourself all those hours poring over newspapers and those crackpot newsletters we pay a small fortune for, written by people who have only one motive in mind – selling their crackpot newsletters. If they really knew what they were talking about, they wouldn't make it public. They'd be cashing in on it for themselves."

That little lecture changed nothing. Zyg had made an exception for Winnipeg in the early days of introducing a different way of doing business. The new model had proved itself. The time had come to have a uniform approach for the whole company.

Cross had had some luck over his career identifying junior oil stocks, companies in the early stages of development. The clients who took his "recommendations" made some good profits. Other than that, the only thing Cross the Barber seemed to excel at, as mentioned, was giving "bean shaves" to clients buying or selling bonds.

■ ■ ■

Perhaps, though, Cross's tonsorial ways were the catalyst for my involvement. My brother, Roi, and I had merged our company, Swasont Brothers & Mayham Inc., into Sheardon-Cassidy after Zyg left and we took over running the company. When the market plunged in the dot.com fiasco, Eldred Donnis convinced his partners to sell IED to Federal Wealth. That left me with nothing to do.

I started up my own little one-man shop as a financial consultant complete with a website and business cards. Sometime after that I emailed an announcement of my new company to everybody I could think of. A cousin of mine from Vancouver, the retiring CFO of WestInvest Investment Services, phoned to see if I knew of anyone in my part of the country who might be interested in a merging with his firm.

WestInvest had its head office in Vancouver, with three other branches in British Columbia and three more in Alberta. Their clients held more than $6 billion in their accounts, "assets under management" in industry talk. It struck me that if Zyg had any intention of becoming a truly national organization, WestInvest would make an excellent stepping stone.

As I might have guessed, Zyg took his time responding to my phone call. I suspect that had something to do with a deal Zyg and I worked on together several years before, back in his Sutton Securities days, that went sour when the real-estate developer involved skipped town along with his secretary and some of the capital we had raised for an intended condo development.

Zyg's voice was less than welcoming when he finally did return my call, as if I were after him for a charitable donation or had another bad deal in mind. But when I presented my idea of beefing up IED's presence in the West, he set up a breakfast meeting with me for the next morning, right after his yoga class. Obviously, he liked the idea. He was fully confident his business model world would work as well in the West as it had started to in Toronto. With IED's limited capital and WestInvest's stubbornness over price, the deal almost fell through twice. So when I suggested a special share arrangement that guaranteed WestInvest owners would get their money if their company generated the kind of revenue they projected, that saved the day – and the deal. Overnight, IED Securities grew by 30 percent, and in certain parts of Manitoba, was thought to be too big for its britches.

During the ups and downs of the negotiation, Zyg and I met three or four times each week and exchanged text messages and phone calls by the dozen. Though I didn't play squash (or pretend tennis), that was overcome by the fact that we were both serious baseball fans. Four or five times we found a way to catch a few innings of a ball game. He began to trust me more and more. He liked the way I could get quickly to the heart of the matter.

Looking back, I see now that slowly I became a surrogate for his friend Harvey who, Zyg concluded, would never return to an environment that tolerated the presence of Dr. Leon Kelpner, D.D.S, Dip. Perio., or Mr. Lawrence Lipakowski, the two who had taken over the investment counselling firm where Harvey worked. (Harvey's observation was that the regulators shouldn't have allowed those two individuals to manage anything larger than a mid-sized car wash.) So, in a way, I had taken on Harvey's role as father confessor. Zygmunt needed someone to talk to. He and I fell into the habit of having dinner once a week, often at Thrace's.

He'd forgiven me for the condo deal that had fallen apart many years before and dropped his nickname for me, Ferdy Fkup. At dinner we talked about business, baseball, and in an exceedingly open way about his past with Antoinette. I didn't know her at all. Frankly, she seemed to me somewhat haughty, a characteristic not uncommon to Montrealers – what other kind of demeanour would you expect from people who call a high hill in the middle of their city a mountain?

Getting IED on the right track and in a new direction was a seven-day-a-week, eighty-hour-a-week affair. Zyg was bound to lose some of his devil-may-care ways. He was determined to make a success of IED and change the way at least one house on The Street did business to a "fairer and more compassionate" way.

Being a victim, too, of the Save Your Time Software Co. (now referred to on The Street as FIAS Co), I knew he'd lost considerable money on it. When it was still in beta testing, a rival company from La Hoya, California, backed by billionaire Justin Quincy-Fox, brought to market Justin Time Solutions with a multi-million-dollar marketing campaign. And that was that. I lost a fair packet and so did Eldred Donnis. But I got the impression that Zyg lost a lot more than he could afford to. So I thought his need to get his financial situation healthy was the origin of his determination to turn IED into a major "player" on Bay Street. From what I know now, though, I can say his motivation was, as motives usually are, much more complex.

The addition of the western offices meant Zyg had to spend more time on the road and less at Admiral Crescent. Often business forced one or the other of its residents to cancel dinner (not Woof-Woof, of course) or skip a movie or play. Lizzy-Anne never seemed to mind even when they had to cut short the seven days they were to spend in Puerto Vallarta.

A nice thing about the "Big Pharma" alliance: it had no goals. The live-in arrangement was something drifted into more by accident than from passion: a three-day national sales meeting at her office became much simpler if Lizzy-Anne stayed at Admiral Crescent and cut her commuting time of an hour and a half (on good days) from north of the city to a pleasant ten-minute walk. That three-night stay was extended into fourteen months. The alliance had no marked beginning. There was no six-month or one-year anniversary to celebrate. Nor did it have any sense of commitment. It just meant more and more clothes in the guest room closet and more cosmetics, cosmetic devices, and other accoutrements in the medicine cabinet in the guest bathroom. The relationship had no ups or downs, no huffs, no puffs, not one "how could you?" Zyg's ardour was never refused or demanded. The "Big Pharma" period, that little ménage à trois, might have gone on – who knows how long? – had Zyg not noticed one night at Thrace's on the other side of the room, gold-incrusted buttons aligned along the cuffs and collars of a white jacket.

Before the week was out, Lizzy-Anne agreed to move to a furnished two-bedroom sublet in an attractive building right around the corner from the Faskin-Allied office. Zyg's offer to pay for the move and the first year's rent might have had an influence. By 10:15 the following Saturday morning, Lizzy-Anne was gone from Admiral Crescent. And, since the daytime dog walker had enrolled full-time at the university, it only made sense for Lizzy-Anne to take Woof-Woof along with her. It would be easy for her to slip home at noon to take the dog for a walk or get someone in her office to do it.

At 10:17 Zygmunt was on the phone. "Oh, hi! Hi, Aunt Sally! It's Zygmunt. Zygmunt Adams?" he said, raising his voice on *Adams*.... Yes, that Zygmunt. Sorry. Sorry to be so slow getting back to you.... Yes, you're right, it's almost a year. Yes, you're right, does seem a tad tardy on my part."

9

FastHorses

June 2005

"You guys can't be serious. I'd have to be out of my frigging mind to get involved in something like that. A horse-breeding farm? You kidding? Horse farms are nothing but sinkholes for money. I'd be smarter to buy an airline. Lose my dough slower. And, shit, I'm just starting to get my head above water and all my stupid loans paid off. When you've made as many turkey investments as I have, you hope you get a little smarter.

"The two of you've got a wonderful, wonderful idea here. I'm not saying you don't, not for a second. But a great idea is one thing. It's another thing to make it work. A horse farm? I'd have to be out of my head. Completely stark-raving goddamn nuts. As it is, my friend Harvey questions my sanity these days. If he heard of this, me getting involved in a wild scheme like this, he'd tell me to get myself committed. I'm not kidding. No, I think you two fine gentlemen will have to count me out on this one. Thanks for showing me the deal. And I wish you all the luck in the world. No two guys in the world deserve a break more than you guys. If there's some other way I can help …"

That's what Zyg would have liked to have said to any two people who approached him about a partnership in a horse farm, any two other than Lance Warburton and His Worship, Billy Mayer.

After all, His Worship had launched Zyg's career, putting the pension account for the Horsemen's Protective Society in Zyg's care back in the early days at Sutton with Marty Pursutto breathing down his neck, bad breath and all. And the reason Zyg knew His Worship in the first place was thanks to Lance, the only person to befriend Zyg when he started out as the assistant head dishwasher, a time when he didn't know another soul at Woodbine, or for that matter another soul in the whole country.

Zyg should have had the two men come to Admiral Crescent, but they were anxious to meet, so he slid them in for twenty minutes between meetings at 370 Bay. Out of habit, both men offered to take their boots off before entering Zyg's office. Zyg persuaded them it wasn't necessary and guided them to a table over by the window. As he sat down, Lance looked around and commented that the office was large enough for a small paddock.

Lance and His Worship started in on their proposal with all the enthusiasm and confidence of owners whose horse had just won the Triple Crown. His Worship was out of a job. New blood at the Horsemen's Protective Society had voted him out of office; they felt he was too close to the owners and trainers and not supportive enough of the jockeys and the stable workers. Lance had wanted to own a farm from when he had first got bitten by the racing bug at eighteen.

"That got us to thinking," Lance said. "And we looked at farms everywhere within a hundred miles of the city. They all cost a fortune, except Silverbrooke, and it has everything we need. The place needs work, sure. An acre costs a song there because it's nowhere. We're the only two guys in the world could make it work there. His Worship's got the reputation, the connections, the clout. People trust him. Even I trust him." He elbowed his partner. "He wasn't the second-best trainer in the province for nothing the year he took on the presidency of the society. He has a feel for young horses. God gives you that. You don't learn it. And, of course, nobody in these parts knows bloodlines better than me. You've seen that yourself at the track dozens of times. You can't be a successful handicapper like me and not know bloodlines. This is a once in a lifetime –"

His Worship interrupted. "They're some sweet tax deductions in all this. And when the economy goes bad, there are still big spenders around with big dough for horses. Back when the pension fund was in the sewer, good horses still fetched really fancy sums. And if you ask Lance himself who can run a better stable than Lance, you'll get a big smile, and braggart that he is, he'll tell you nobody. I swear he can trace a horse's lineage all the way back to the Darley Arabian or the Byerley Turk. You can't run a decent breeding operation unless some-body knows their genealogy. And, Zyg, on top of that, no two guys on God's earth have a greater love of horses than Lance and me. No two. You know that."

His Worship brought out a spreadsheet showing the "sources and uses" of capital for the first three years of operation. Zyg scanned it quickly. He didn't believe the numbers for a second.

"Hard to see how an operation like this could miss," Zyg said, but without enthusiasm.

Even though the stock market was moving up strongly, the three founders of the FastHorses Breeding and Racing Corporation of Canada ("TFHBRCC," as the documents of incorporation referred to their new operation, incorporated under the Canada Business Corporations Act) were unable to attract even one other investor. And they tried hard, very hard, approaching almost everybody around the track who they thought had $10,000 or more available for such a venture or adventure.

TFHBRCC issued three common shares, one to each participant. The capital needed over and above the mortgage on the farm came from the preferred shares issued to the participants in return for cash. In the case of Lance and His Worship, the cash came from the sale of their city homes, and in Zyg's case, a much larger amount, from the sale of some stocks Kopsin sold and a drawdown from the home equity loan on Admiral Crescent.

Although "Silverbrooke was nowhere and you could buy an acre for a song," as the proposers suggested, that wasn't quite the price shown in the spreadsheet for one hundred and twenty-six acres with its buildings and equipment, including the latest Equicizer, which any efficient, first-rate operation had to have. There was a stable that housed three dozen horses, a large barn, a five-eighths-of-a-mile turf track and a half-mile dirt track, each with a starting gate, two houses, and a half-dozen paddocks. His Worship, a widower, moved into the smaller house almost immediately. Within a month the other house was ready for Lance and his wife as the population of Silverbrooke, a thriving lumber town a hundred years before, swelled to twenty-nine.

■ ■ ■

If she didn't have too many files on the go, Antoinette accompanied Zyg out to FastHorses for the management meetings the first and third Sunday of the month but on one condition: she drove in her Volvo. She took exactly the same route as Zyg, winding through the same back streets to get on the fourteen-lane 401 expressway out of the city and then sliding off onto quieter two-lane highways and eventually onto tree-lined concession roads that ran past fields tilled brown or sprouting young green crops.

The trip out to Silverbrooke took her an hour and forty minutes, a good twenty minutes longer than Zyg. When they got there and got out of the car, Antoinette stretched her arms up at the sky and took large gulps of the clean air. Her (almost constant) sardonic half smile broke into a full smile and brought softness to her face. On these occasions, Zygmunt went over to Lance's house for the meeting, while Antoinette walked to the stables, sometimes skipping for a step or two like a child on the way home from school.

When she got to the stables, she greeted each horse by name and with a pat on its head. Lance's horse was always waiting and saddled. She took it for long rides along the trails around the property and in the adjacent woods. After the first month, though, Zyg bought her a beautiful blond-maned Palomino, which he named One Smart Biscuit. If the meeting was still on when she got back from her ride, she sat in the tack room and read whatever book she'd brought along.

By the spring of the following year, 2006, FastHorses was in full operation with a stable of a dozen and half horses (two fillies, bought as yearlings, had shown exceptional speed in their workouts). Some of the horses weren't true residents. They were bought at the fall auction to be worked with over the winter and then sold in the spring to generate cash. To the surprise of all three members of the management team, the revenue and expenses for the first months weren't far off those in the spreadsheet presented in Zyg's Ballroom Office.

Driving out one day, Antoinette complained about the steep increase in the maintenance fees for her condo.

"Antoinette, you're just throwing your money out the door. It should be going into your Independence Fund."

"You see that creep pass me on the hill?"

"Why not move into Admiral Crescent?" This was a subject Zyg hadn't brought up for some time.

"That would imply you and I were serious."

"Be more of a dress rehearsal."

"A dress rehearsal for real life? That's absurd."

"Well, then, marry me. Forget the rehearsal."

"I like being with you, Zyg." Her hand came off the steering wheel for a few seconds and stroked his thigh. "I like spending time together. But one day we'd bicker and you'd ask me to leave just like you did Big Pharma and … and my dog."

"It's different. I'm in love with you. You know that."

"No, I don't. I honestly don't. I have a lot of trouble frankly seeing how a card-carrying womanizer like you would know what love was about in the first place."

"I know I love my neighbour."

"She's a hundred and eight."

"Ninety-two. But I love her. I take flowers and chocolates over to her all the time. And I keep an eye on her place when she visits her son and the grandchildren in Los Angeles."

"Why don't you marry her? The two of you could get a nice place in Palm Springs. Her grandchildren are probably your age. You'd have someone to play with."

"You're a tougher negotiator than my people in Winnipeg, Mademoiselle Mairie."

"You're a lovely man, Zyg. You are. You have a wonderful spirit. But experience tells me guys like you never change. That past is a pretty good indicator of future performance."

"What do you mean guys like me?"

"I don't think I really ever told you about my first so-called love." Antoinette brought the car to a dead stop and looked both ways twice before crossing the side road. "My last year at McGill I moved in with a much older guy. I was mad about him. He was a broker like you, a broker to a bunch of Westmount snobs he grew up with. At least that was his day job. His name was Randy. I used to call him Randy the Dandy. He was always dressed to the nines, never a hair on his head out of place.

"He and his buddies had a pickup hockey game every Thursday night. One Thursday, the night before my very last exam, I got through at the library a little early. Instead of going back to the apartment, a classmate and I went to a bar on Crescent Street for a nightcap. And that Thursday night who should be sitting at a table large as life? None other than my Dandy old Randy. With a woman. And he wasn't holding a hockey stick. He was holding her hand. The bastard was holding her hand. I can still picture it. I realized immediately he was a broker during the day, all right, but after work he was a test pilot for a zipper factory.

"He didn't see me. When he got home, I pretended to be asleep. The next day he was off to some mutual fund conference for the weekend. I wrote my exam – I don't know how – and moved out. My note to him said never to contact me again – never. I left Montreal and never went back, not even for graduation. I don't know how I ever got over that. I really don't. I lived in a community of one for a long, long time."

"How old were you?" Zyg asked.

"Twenty-one. Twenty–two. That ever happen to you?"

"Sort of. It's starting to rain. Want me to drive?"

"No, much easier on my nerves if I do. How much farther?"

"Good half an hour."

"You know what gets me? With you guys, as far as I can tell, you never know whether a deal is a merger or an acquisition. Twice I thought I was in a merger. Wrong. Dead wrong both times. They were acquisitions. That isn't happening again." She pronounced each word slowly. "That isn't happening again. Ever. I'm not into subservience. Believe me, I'm totally ... fiercely ... not into subservience."

"For God's sake, Antoinette, if I didn't know that by now, I'd never have gotten out of grade school."

"It took me forever to get over Randy the Dandy. I cried for months. Medications didn't help a bit. But in the end it turned out to be a good thing. That's why I went into family law.

"With the Combatant, it was different. We spent a long time getting to know each other. He was a marketing consultant. Strategies, logos, brilliant tag lines, clever PR, smart ads – all that crap. He used to tell me how successful branding wasn't about building emotional attachments and massaging expectations. Those were only the tricks used to get you to stop thinking and hand over your trust. When they ask you what'll you have to drink, you want your customer to respond automatically – without thinking – 'A Coke' or 'A Bud' or 'Espresso Grande.' A mother's love is natural across all species.

"After the Randy episode, I read a lot about love. A lot. Not about parental love – that seems natural to all animals, not just us. Just because we use the same name for different kinds of love doesn't mean they're the same thing, any more than two people with the same name means there's only one person. Unlike the others, love between two adults – call it romantic love, if you like – is a concoction, a social concoction. Like I told you in New York at that marvellous restaurant, it's all a branding job."

The conversation began to feel like New York all over again. Like a cold front moving in from the Arctic. It seemed every time Zyg pressed Antoinette to make any kind of commitment, she turned to books, as if they could tell her what to feel or how to think about love. But unlike New York, Zyg didn't quit. Quitting this time, he knew, would mean the end – for good.

"Ah, Antoinette," Zyg almost pleaded, "I'm like you. Looking for something with some stability to it. We aren't kids anymore, you know."

"Love's just a word. What does it mean when somebody says 'I love you'? Is it the same sort of thing as loving your stamp collection? Something you take up or put down whenever you feel like it? Words work just like brands – they hide as much as they reveal, often more."

"I've always liked numbers," Zyg said. "If somebody says three, you know pretty well what they mean." He was trying, but it wasn't working. Antoinette wouldn't be deterred.

"With the Combatant I was sure we had love going for us. But – and maybe this is my real point – I was wrong. And what's so terrible about that is that's what I get to see every day almost. Women – men – in my office telling me if they were in love, they say, they sure as hell aren't anymore or their partner isn't. They got fooled. Whatever the word *love* suggested to them wasn't what they got. Words lie. They lie like a trooper. When I look *love* up in the dictionary, the only definition that makes sense to me is: 'in tennis, no points.'"

"Well, you don't give up in tennis just because you're behind a few points."

"People don't get it. Love's not just an emotion. It's more like a process, a state of mind, a way of being. Sex is just the liftoff part. Lots of flames and sparks and smoke. But when the smoke clears, guess what gets left on the launching pad most of the time. The love. 'Hello, Mission Control? Mission Control? Something's wrong here – Billy's gone and buggered off!'"

"That's what your books tell you? What do they know? In my business, people who write books on how to make money know only one way to make money – selling their books. If they really knew how to make money in the market, they'd be out there doing it, not writing about it."

"I agree. As far as I can tell, most of the people who write about love, the poets and the songwriters and the psycho-folks, are either delusional or pandering to the marketplace."

"Maybe we each have our own kind of love. Each a little different. This brand a little more kind. That one a little more demanding. This one a little more compassionate. That one more possessive. What I'm promoting today is the Zyg brand. A superior, leading-edge kind of love – with a lifetime guarantee thrown in."

"But that's my point. How do you know the guarantee is any good? It could be a knock-off."

What could Zyg say? He shrugged and was at a loss for words. But he didn't give up. He just smiled.

As they drove through the gateway of FastHorses, Antoinette relented. "Zyg I wouldn't be around if I wasn't fond of you. But I don't know if I ever did love. Or if I did, could again. After two giant disasters, I don't know if I can trust me, let alone you. There's a definite limit to the amount of disappointment a heart can accept."

"I'm doing my damnedest to show you ... to show you can."

Antoinette glanced up at him. She had to smile. She, too, had run out of words, so she took Zyg's hand, brought it to her face, and kissed it. "You know what? Next time we drive out here I'm bringing a talking book for us."

10
Ascending

In the three years since Kopsin T. Shurtz had taken over as IED's chief investment officer and chief equity strategist, though the climb had been far from smooth, the stock markets in North America had risen 50 percent. That made him – or helped make him – look like a hero. Nobody could criticize his selection of stocks over that period, not even Cross Bennett, who could find no explanation other than pure luck as to why, or how, a former compliance officer could make so many successful calls in a row.

Skly Cszymorska, who had stayed on as head of research, mostly oversaw the conversion of new clients' portfolios, a process that could take more than a year, since Kopsin liked to "feather" money gently out of the old holdings and into the IED "pooled" funds. Don-Phil de Vita, the senior vice-president of sales, had left some time ago to take over marketing for a hedge fund firm of contrarian investors ("Integrity. Capital Preservation. Un-herd Intelligence").

Nadia Whitall had come up with one good idea after another. Shortly after her arrival, IED brought on staff a tax specialist and set up relationships with estate lawyers, divorce specialists, tax preparers, accountants, actuaries, employment counsellors, retirement counsellors, insurance and risk advisers, succession consultants, an elder-care consultant, and even a funeral director, thanks, of course, to Skly's connections to the investor relations manager for Pluman's. At her suggestion, too, the management committee made annual checkups at

ExecuMed Health Services mandatory for all of IED's senior officers and managers.

And thanks to Nadia the account executives now talked more about the "service experience" than they did about winners and losers. Though even the bank-owned firms tried in their way to copy this approach years later, no other firm on The Street at that time had anything like the number of different services available to look after the needs of its clients or prospective clients.

Time and timing can explain many things. After the markets "headed south big-time" in 2001, 2002, and 2003, many investors felt discouraged and disenchanted with The Street. On top of that, the over-fifty demographic had begun to discover Google and the wonders of searching the Internet. Nadia got her nephew, Crackle Fanning, to build a website for IED with the tag line "Quiet Investing." The timing to introduce a digital marketing campaign couldn't have been better. Within a few weeks, after it was launched, dozens of email inquiries flowed in from the disenchanted who had just "taken a bath – big-time."

Under Zyg's leadership, IED thrived as it had never before in its thirty-seven years of prestigiousness. The total amount of money held in clients' accounts ("assets under administration," in Street lingo) quadrupled. Joan-e and her crowd moved over from Sutton, and IED began to steal business from investment counsellors and mutual funds alike. And that didn't go unnoticed by The Street.

A sense of pride grew among IEDers. Slowly into their bar chatter entered the claim of IED being the best house on The Street to work for. And even when the market took dips, which might last months, you would still hear laughter in the Back Office and, say, absurd jokes about replacing two-year-old carpets when somebody spilled coffee (in former days, carpets would have had to grow mould first). Zyg's hard work and eighty-hour weeks paid off. IED was now a force on The Street. People, referred by IED's own clients, were phoning in to set up appointments. Some clients from other houses, including even Federal Wealth, were moving without even waiting to hear about the company's philosophy – an unheard of phenomenon in a space where the be-all and end-all for gaining new clients was "Sell, sell, sell." At least according to one observer.

January 2007

Some people swear no greater curse can befall a person, no matter the field – sports, hospitality, show business, finance – than to be selected as the outstanding representative of that field for the year.

Zyg held no such superstitions about what fate had in store for the sports teams he bet on, nor the horses, nor about the licence plate number on his car, nor about the women who chose to have congress with him. He didn't believe in omens of any kind with one exception: his regular handouts to bring luck to Segovia, the street mendicant who showed up at the southeast corner of Bay and King each Friday night to strum on a stringless guitar.

Segovia would strum – and hum – his *Arrivederci Concerto* for the citizens fleeing The Street for the weekend with the hope of diverting some of the week's cash flow from their pockets into his. A peek at his open, red-lined guitar case suggested only limited success.

So Zyg saw no harm at all in being chosen by *The Sage Adviser*, the industry's highly regarded trade magazine, as Wealth Management Executive of 2006 and to be celebrated at the King Edward Hotel. By then Zyg and Antoinette had been back together (though that might not be quite the right expression) for more than a year and a half.

Antoinette arrived late. I saw her come in the door, but the pillars in the converted banquet room made it almost impossible for her to see me. I got up and brought her over to our table as *The Sage Adviser*'s editor explained his choice.

"He worked tirelessly to introduce new ways to wealth management operations, changing, to use his words, his firm from a sales organization to a service organization. As anybody in this game knows, changing your business model is no easy task. Investing is a very complex business – and getting more complex by the day. One simple example comes to mind. Twenty years ago you could publish the tax act in a book of four hundred pages and it sold for less than $25. Today fifteen hundred pages are required to capture all the rules, and it costs at least a hundred bucks. The computer has changed everything. That meant our industry had to change. We had to find new and better ways to do things.

"The winner of our award recognized that. He redesigned his company. And while most firms have found it difficult to get back up to speed, his firm, in three years, went all the way from fourth quartile to first in our annual survey of customer service in the wealth management industry. In fact, his company received the highest satisfaction ranking – 9.45 – ever.

"As an aside, his company was the first to get a perfect ten-out-of-ten rating for the quality of the statements they send clients. We don't know all the secret ingredients in his formula, but if we're lucky, tonight he'll tell us some. His leadership skills, some people say, saved his company. Perhaps he can save other wealth managers. Ladies and gentlemen, may I introduce to you …"

Up on her feet, clapping away, was Antoinette. But to this day, I don't think she ever realized how much of an influence she and her skepticism played in Zyg's award.

The write-up the next day in Halvert Tulvin's "Goings-On" in *The World of Finance* helped convince the WestInvest branch managers they had joined the right team. The changeover had been far from easy. Some valued clients (to use a Street cliché) left. But when the portfolios of all but the most cautious clients jumped 12 percent or better in the first year after the acquisition (referred to by *The World of Finance* as a "merger"), WestInvest's people were won over.

The staff in those offices preferred working with the demanding Zyg in place of their former president, who showed more interest in tracking how many pencils went missing every week. They much preferred working with a service mentality rather than the old who-can-we-get-to-buy-what-today attitude. One broker claimed not having to meet a quota every quarter was like drawing a permanent get-out-of-jail-free card in Monopoly. If a client asked about some obscure tax point, you could get a response back from Toronto within a day. And with equal promptness, Skly and his research department provided you with reliable information on even the most obscure stock.

People taking more credit than they deserved wasn't unknown on The Street. For example, in Federal Wealth's annual report, the CEO unhesitatingly took credit for every nickel of the increase in revenue and profit. Whereas we all know that success, if not all human behaviour, is the product of an infinite number of factors, and picking out just one or even two usually oversimplifies how human events evolve.

In the case of IED's newfound prosperity, Zyg's leadership was a major factor, no question. But the rising stock market and Kopsin's unusual ability to exploit it helped a great deal. Talk about magic. As if to make up for all the ill health inflicted upon the poor man, nature seemed to have bestowed Mr. Shurtz with the visionary skills of an astute shaman. To repeat, even Cross Bennett, in his long career, had never seen anything quite like it, though he remained adamant that Winnipeg had no need of Kopsin's suggestions. To keep the peace, Zyg compromised, though not without regret. All Winnipeg's new clients had to be serviced with the new model. The old clients, Winnipeg could convert in its own time.

Everything else around IED and FastHorses seemed, like Segovia, to be humming along.

11
Descending

For Kopsin, 2007 got off to a great start. In his first bridge tournament, he added eight-tenths of a point to the nineteen hundred and thirty "master points" he had already earned. The following Thursday with more master points within his grasp, an opponent on his left, a young, plumpish Filipina, an off-duty ICU nurse he had never seen around the bridge club before, opened play with a singleton king of spades, the only lead that could defeat his six no-trump contract. Intrigued and emboldened, after the scores were tallied up and not even a fraction of a master point awarded him, he invited that opponent for a drink.

He followed that up with the suggestion they grab a quick bite of dinner at Guy Ding's before the next bridge session. And then he invited her to theatre the first night she was off-duty again and they weren't playing bridge. On a Friday afternoon, four weeks later, the two bridge players teamed up at City Hall.

Zyg stood up as the best man and Antoinette as the maid of honour. The two attendants claimed the smile on Kopsin's face took up half the judge's chambers, the other half occupied by the smile on the face of the newest Mrs. Shurtz. The other Mrs. Shurtz, Kopsin's mother, declined to attend the ceremony. She told Kopsin he was "pushing his luck."

The World of Finance picked up the story of Kopsin's marriage and took it as a reason to profile IED's success and how quickly the company had "rocketed" to the top of the mid-tier financial houses in the country.

But, in fact, Zyg's business model was losing fuel.

As always, there were clients (usually doctors) who felt they could outsmart the market, especially when it came to industries they knew nothing about such as gold mining. IED had to accommodate clients like that who insisted on playing the market (though company policy dictated that account executives had to send such clients the Ritson, Solder, Blakley et al. study, which claimed to show that very few short-term traders actually turned a profit). Stock trades initiated by someone other than Kopsin or Skly were known around IED as "H and P's" – "Hope and Prayer" purchases – mostly to buy or sell "hot" stocks. Over the previous three years, such trades had dropped from 83 percent of the volume to less than 15 percent, most of those coming from long-time clients in Winnipeg and Portage la Prairie.

The previous summer Kopsin had become suspicious of the U.S. housing market. Even though in the fall of that year, 2006, the stocks of home builders shot up, he became distrustful of the market. He didn't like what his charts told him. And he didn't like the growing number of mortgages in default nor the increase in home prices without an accompanying increase in sales.

Slowly, he switched clients from stocks into safe short-term govern-ment bonds and treasury bills and even into cash. But the more cautious Kopsin became, the higher the markets headed. In early January, just before he met his wife-to-be, he reduced clients' stock exposure even more. So while Kopsin was courting, marrying, and perhaps for the first time in his life, making love, some people around IED were preparing for war.

Memories are short. Some clients and a few of IED's account execu-tives forgot all the smart moves Kopsin had made over the previous three years. By March 2007, before the daffodils and tulips began to sprout in the flower beds of Old City Hall up the street, buds of discon-tent started to germinate in Zyg's emails, a new crop almost every day as the markets climbed their way to new highs.

We all have days when the world seems to fit together: when you find a parking spot in front of your dentist's office, when a newly installed software app performs without a hitch, and when a kitchen drawer holds exactly the right tool to loosen the recalcitrant lid on a jar of pickles. Those are beautiful days, faith enhancers. Then there's an opposite kind of day:

Sent: 14/03/2007 11:37 a.m.
From: c.bennett@ ied.ca
To: z.adams@ied.ca
Subject: A Problem

Zyg, do you mind if I ask what the hell you guys are doing down there? My clients are doing just fine, thank you very much. They're making good dough. But your compliance officer genius down there has had my reps' people in bonds that earn about 2 percent a year at best. My clients make more than that in a month. To be frank, our reps aren't happy. In fact, they t'ain't happy at all. We aren't looking good.

Could you, please, have a serious chat with our chief investment officer before we go up in flames because we missed out on one of the best bull markets in years?

PLEASE!

Yours faithfully,

Cross

Disclaimer: This email is intended only for the named recipient(s) above and may contain information that is privileged, confidential, and/or exempt from disclosure under applicable law. If you have received this message in error, or are not the named recipient(s), please immediately notify the sender and permanently delete this email message and any attachments without retaining a copy. Please do not print this email unless necessary.

Then there was another email forwarded by an account executive in the Toronto office:

Sent: 11/3/2007 11:37 a.m.
From: J. Smeed [mailto:jsmeed@ied.ca]
To: zyg.adams@ied.ca
Subject: Important

Zyg, see below.

Jason.

_____

Sent: 5/3/2007 11:37 a.m.
From: G.A. de Fainéant [mailto: gdefaineant@uhn.ca]
To: J. Smeed [mailto: jsmeed@ied.ca]
Subject: He-LLO!!!

Jason, I moved my account over to your shop last summer. I was attracted by your track record. But here I am now up to my elbows in stupid T-bills and government bonds that earn me next to nothing. My urological colleague across the hall just raked in twenty-two grand on Westwood Forest Products and another twelve grand on RBC Septic Devices and Tanks. You talked me out of both of those deals. If a urologist can make money in this market, believe me, anybody can.

I am seriously considering moving back to where I came from. Please advise me why I shouldn't. Looks to me like I have badly misdiagnosed your company's skills.

Yours,

George Angus de Fainéant, M.D., F.R.C.P., Dip. Stk.

By no means was this unhappiness confined to the digital world, which had become so efficient at spreading dissent and discontentment.

"I don't know," said an account exec to Toddy Landau sitting around the boardroom just before the monthly "Shoptalk" meeting with Nadia. "I hate it when my clients are out of the market and the goddamn thing rockets up. And they hate it, too. I don't know about this guy Shurtz. Whenever you ask him a question, you can't understand a word he says. He rattles off all these arguments, statistics, and then ends up saying 'Maybe.' What kind of bullshit is that? What am I supposed to tell my clients? If they ask should they put more dough in the market, am I supposed to say, 'Maybe'? That would be a winner. We used to be so positive about the market around here. Nobody ever mentions 'buying opportunities' anymore when dips come along. The market goes down, sure, but sooner or later, it'll come back up again. Sooner or later. It always has. And it always will."

At one point or another many highly regarded money managers have found themselves out of touch with the market. For one, the legendary Julian Robertson closed out his Tiger Fund in 2000, thanks to the bankruptcy of US Airways. Helen Young Hayes, Morningstar's International Fund Manager of 1997, who Kopsin admired for years, floundered with the collapse of Enron and the dot.com market, and one of her funds, according to the *Los Angeles Times*, lost 22 percent in one year. And, of course, let's not forget the oft-quoted, oft-appearing guru, Big Bobby Little, former chief equity strategist (and CEO) of IED. In all those cases, people lost money – lots of it. With the new version of IED, no client lost a penny, not a penny. But they weren't making money like their friends boasted about at cocktail parties or around the office.

As stock prices increased, so, in almost perfect correlation, did the criticisms of Kopsin T. Shurtz and his supposed skills. While he himself seemed happier than anyone had ever seen him before, more than one account exec speculated that Kopsin's recent discovery of sex had distorted his view of the markets. That wouldn't have been the first time on The Street that passion overcame clear judgment (at least in the view of one observer). At the monthly IED management meeting the usually unflappable, imperturbable, cool-headed Zygmunt flared: "What the hell are you talking about? The day anyone around here or around The Street can show me that he or she understands markets better than Kopsin, let me know. I want to put my dough with whoever the hell that is."

But Zyg did agree to speak to Kopsin. When the IED CEO went to Kopsin's office later that day, the man, as usual, was poring over his charts. But instead of coughing, he was quietly humming "Fly Me to the Moon."

"Kops, this place looks in about as bad shape as that hole you had over at Sutton," said Zyg. "You've got more charts going here than your wife probably has over in her ICU unit. How's she doing, by the way?"

"Terrific! She's having such a good time. We went to Niagara Falls on the weekend for a second two-day honeymoon. We both won at black-jack. We're going to the ballet tonight. Toddy gave me some tickets. We get to do bridge at least once a week. Never play together, though. That would be pushing my luck."

"That's wonderful to hear."

"So far, so good. I should have done it years ago. You know what I never realized? I was so busy watching hockey and baseball that I never realized how much fun it is to have someone to watch with."

"I have to ask, are you still convinced the markets are in for trouble?"

"That's my best guess. What I'm guessing right now is clients will do better out of the market than in. Housing in the U.S. looks very, very soft to me. And if it goes down, lots of other things go down with it – jobs, refrigerators, furnaces, softwood lumber."

"Should we be looking at Asia or Europe, some other places in the world to invest in? Some of the folks are getting a little restless."

"When things fall apart, a lot of people are going to get hurt. Just like in the dot-com days. Too much debt around. Far too much. Everybody'll rush into cash. Liquidity. Liquidity. Liquidity. But whenever The Street wants to get liquid, things get messy as hell. Maybe even messier. I've never seen hell."

"Any idea how long it could go on for before things start to go south?"

"Nope, no idea. That's the problem. Could happen tomorrow, a month from now, six months. You can tell if the dam needs repair, but not when it's going to burst. One thing – the longer this goes on, the farther we'll fall. Clients just have to be patient."

"Easy for a happily married equity strategist to say," Zyg said, sighing. Later that day an email went off:

Sent: 16/3/2007 5:15 p.m.
From: z.adams@ied.ca
To: IED
Subject: What's Going On?

CONFIDENTIAL: FOR IED PERSONNEL ONLY.

Over the past three years, not many on The Street have had a better investment record than our chief strategist. Many of our clients have seen their portfolios double or better in that time. And many of you have seen huge increases in the assets under your care thanks to his calls on the North American markets. But we all know markets don't go up forever. Has everybody forgotten post-2000 already?

Our strategy at this point is to position clients conservatively until things settle down. As Kopsin explained to me today, there are times when playing it safe is the best thing to do. Of course, you understand that. You're professional advisers. But that doesn't mean your clients will. We will help you explain it in every way we can. That's our job. And your job.

Zyg.

■ ■ ■

"Sorry, I'm not much fun tonight in bed or out," Antoinette told Zyg during an interlude. "I had such a terrible day. I botched a file really badly. That always puts a massive wall between the world and me. Makes me feel so isolated. I thought I could trust this lawyer. I allowed him a postponement. Huge mistake. I should have nailed the little bugger when I had him."

"I hate it when you talk about being lonely."

"Zyg, you're so patient with me. You really are. And I know that's not your style. I appreciate it. I really do. It's taking me such a long time. You'd think I'd be over the Combatant by now. But I seem to have lost all faith in my judgment. I was so sure of myself back then." She moved closer to him.

They had grabbed a quick bite to eat earlier before going off to the opening of *A Penny for Your Thoughts* at the Pump House Theatre around the corner from Zyg's place. After that they'd gone straight to bed.

"Why take your ex-husband as an example of marriage?" Zyg asked. "Take Kopsin instead. God, you should see him around the office these days. He doesn't snivel anymore. He just smiles. He smiles all the time. Today when I walked into his office he was humming. He's a different man." Zyg swung his arm under Antoinette. "If you, the great observer of love, want to see what love looks like, take a look at the Shurtzs. It's beautiful. We'll have dinner with them one night and you'll see."

"There you go again. You're really so Bay Street. You guys jump to conclusions at the drop of a hat. What's it been, three months? He's still in the lust stage. How many fights have they had? None, I bet. Give him a couple of years and then we'll see what tune he's whistling."

"What am I going to do with you, Antoinette? You've become so cynical."

"Zyg, you of all people should know better. How many times did a couple of good rolls in the hay wipe out any thought you had of something durable with one of your many little victims? Poor Kopsin, with all that dopamine and oxytocin and serotonin rolling around in his head, I'll bet his brain has turned into Danish topsoil, as Lance likes to say. You better keep a close eye on him."

"Funny you should say that. Winnipeg and even a couple of account execs around our office are mad as hell at him. They send me these terrible emails. Kopsin's had our clients out of the market virtually for the past six months. But the market keeps going up and up. And these guys keep howling. They think he's lost his touch."

"Was that moral dwarf in Winnipeg after you again?"

"Kopsin knows his stuff. No question. He's a professional. The man eats and sleeps markets and reads annual reports for breakfast, lunch, and dinner. No, if anybody knows what they're doing, lovesick or not, it'd be Kopsin. I'm prepared to wait."

"Kopsin and I are the only two people on this earth you have any patience with. And we both seem to be trying it these days."

"I've waited four years for you."

"Not four years. What about your Big Pharma period?"

"It wasn't that long. Anyway, Kopsin's example shows people can be happily married at least for a while."

"I told you a hundred times I don't marry."

"What do you mean you don't marry? You did marry."

"Once, yes, but I kicked the habit. You and I don't know each other nearly well enough. You forget. What we've got going for us is just a series of one-night stands."

"You stayed with me at Admiral Crescent for three nights straight in the winter."

"You had a bad flu. I didn't want you to go to a hospital. Hospitals are places where sick people go to get sicker."

"You're really serious about that, aren't you?"

"You know I am. They're terrible places. Iatrogenic inns, that's all they are. And drug pushers." Then Antoinette added almost as a footnote to that short debate on the health system: "How about a compromise?"

"You okay? You feeling well? I never heard you use that word before. What kind of compromise?"

"Why don't we go steady?"

"Oh, Antoinette, for God's sake we aren't teenagers anymore."

"Buy me a nice ring. A 'promise' ring, that's what the kids call them now. No diamonds. Nothing expensive. I'll wear it on my little finger and we can go steady and just not live under the same roof. Sort of, you know, kicking it up a notch. Gets us over the hump of all these one-night stands we've been having the past four years."

"That's the craziest thing I ever heard of. What am I supposed to tell them at the office? Break out the beer, guys, and get the boardroom ready for a crap game. Antoinette and I have decided to go steady. At our age, Antoinette, that's nuts, absolutely stark-raving goddamn nuts."

The ring from Canadian Precious Jewellers, owned by a former client of Zyg's, consisted of two strands of gold interlocked in a square knot, a sapphire in the middle. And as if Zyg had scrambled the language once again, the inscription inside read: "From Z to A." The ring was far too big. He had to take it back to the Precious people to get it resized.

April 2007

Antoinette was right about one thing: nothing would shake Zygmunt's faith in Kopsin. At the weekly management meeting Zyg presented the opinions of the chief economists of two major banks and the country's largest insurance company. All three wrote that the markets were vulnerable (though none of them foresaw anything graver than a brief downturn in stock prices). Of course, he could have found support from *Market Smarts*, Barry Knight's newsletter, but most people knew that Barry had predicted a market crash every year since he got it right in 1987. In early April, the market dropped sharply and the flow of electronic wrath subsided. But then out of nowhere arose a new and deadly species of discontent.

Over the winter, the influx of clients slowed down as if someone had installed a stop sign on the front door of Suite 400, 370 Bay Street. The growth in "assets under management" stalled. That produced one of the gravest of all Bay Street sins (right up there with "production insufficiency"): no profit growth. For the first time since the early days when Zyg took over at IED, profit hadn't increased for three straight months in a row.

Yikes!

Before excusing himself from a rare appearance on the monthly management conference call to attend a lesson on putting at the Royal Panamanian Golf Club, Sherwin Chable butted into the conversation. "There's no such thing as no growth. You grow. Or you shrink. The obvious mistake here, gentlemen, is to think we're in business to make money. Any idiot can do that. We call people who do that 'wage earners.' IED Securities, gentlemen, isn't in business to make money. Let's get that straight." He raised his voice and began to shout. "We're in business to make … more money! Not just money! More money! You aren't adding any goddamn value to this company unless you keep making more money and more money. Simple as that."

A short silence followed, then an automated voice announced to the conference-call participants: "Sherwin Chable has left the meeting."

"Jesus," Skly said, "I got really confused. When Chable started on about 'more money,' I thought he was complaining about his knee affliction again for the hundredth time. 'You aren't adding any goddamn value to this company unless you keep making Mormon-knee and Mormon-knee. Simple as that.'"

Edgar, chair of the meeting, sounded confused for a moment, then said, "Well, there we have it. Sherwin has cut out our work for us. What I think our chairman was referring to is the need to keep profits growing. If our wealth management fees aren't growing, we need to diversify. We need to find another stream of revenue. And the name of that undertaking, Skly suggested, should be Project Mormon Knee."

"We never should have gotten out of mergers and acquisitions," Cross Bennett threw in. "That was a big mistake. In this market, we could be making money hand over fist underwriting IPOs."

"We're not in that business, we agreed, because it creates conflicts of interest with clients," Edgar said. "That's the sort of thing I think we want to avoid, according to our business model."

Nadia, the director of service, suggested, "We know our model works. Why not expand to Montreal?"

"Whenever I chat with my colleagues in Quebec," Edgar said, "they beg me not to reopen an office there. They claim it would provide the separatists with reason enough to try for another referendum."

"Well, why don't we take it into the States?" Skly countered. "We could buy somebody in New York. Or how about Hong Kong? Things are really booming over there."

"In Hong Kong I doubt if they even know our stock market exists," Edgar said. "But you know that does suggest we might make some headway in Europe. They see us these days as very much of a safe haven with our political and financial stability. You can't find that in many places in today's world."

Zyg had stayed out of the early fray but now said, "Not a bad idea, Edgar. Could work, you know. But not with retail clients. With institutions. I've got some good connections over there from my Sheardon days. There's a guy I know – Gott de Holger – who could put us in business overnight. He was the chief investment officer at the QRS Bank and is on a first-name basis with everybody over there who's anybody. Gott goes to all the Bilderberg conferences and the Davos Forum. We'd be leveraging Kopsin's brain. I like that. I like that idea a lot. Toddy could be our contact man. He could do most of it from here on the phone and the Net and he likes to travel."

"I like the sound of IED Securities International," Skly added. "Makes us appear much more … substantial."

"WestInvest was the only successful expansion in our long history. We need to be prudent and do our homework. The minute we tried to expand in the past," Edgar said, "the market immediately headed into the toilet."

Edgar's words were superfluous. Project Mormon Knee was under way.

12
Another Word or Two on Love

For the following Wednesday, Zyg had planned a small surprise celebration for Antoinette's birthday. She thought there would be just the two of them, but he had invited Joan-e and me and asked us to show up at Thrace's ahead of time as surprise guests.

The day started out unusually chilly, even for April in Toronto. Downtown, patches of snow remained here and there, remnants of the mounds piled up by ploughs over the winter. But in the early afternoon a swath of warm air swooped in from the south and a thick fog settled over the city. Zyg had to forfeit the surprise part of his plan when his flight back from Montreal got delayed. He sent me a text message and asked me to pick Antoinette up.

Joan-e was to drive in from the country. But shortly after Antoinette and I arrived at the restaurant, the maître d', known to us only as Jimmy's brother (the owner and head chef being Dimitri "Jimmy" Thracymachus), came over to our table. He had a message from Joan-e saying she couldn't make the party because, as he said, "there were many accidents all over."

The fog must have discouraged other diners that night. Only three tables besides ours were taken, a poor turnout even for a Tuesday. Thrace's piano player, who'd had a short liaison with Zyg (which ended in an unfriendly way when he excommunicated himself to Vancouver without a word of goodbye), sang the traditional cocktail lounge songs in a soft, sad, haunting voice that filled the pauses in our conversation.

"I'd like a Rob Roy with Johnnie Black, one cube of ice, and a slice of lemon," Antoinette instructed Jimmy's brother. "No sugar. Not a grain. One ounce of sweet vermouth. And easy on the bitters, please, just a dash."

"Belvedere on the rocks for me, please," I said. "And could you make sure the ice is cold?"

"Okay," Antoinette said to me, "so I'm a little fussy about what I eat and drink. I admit it."

Although we had talked briefly at cocktail parties, at *The Sage Adviser*'s Executive of the Year dinner, and on one occasion at the races, Antoinette and I had never had a serious conversation. I knew quite a bit about her, you can be sure, from Zyg when he and I had dinner together. He'd talk about her, holding little if anything back.

Like Zyg, I had always admired her smile, which suggested she was either readying a clever retort or refusing to take seriously whatever was being said to her. She kept others at a distance, whether out of shyness, wariness, or aloofness, I could never determine. And I didn't remember seeing her before in a sleeveless dress and certainly had never noticed how smooth and sensuous her freckled skin was. To fall in love – however you define that event – would have been the last thought on my mind that night, I swear.

"Is that new?" I asked.

"What?"

"The ring. It's quite lovely."

"Zyg and I are going steady. The ring makes it official. Zyg gave it to me a couple of weeks ago." She held out her hand again. "Mind you, I had to ask him for it. Some people will think we're off to Bermuda on Sunday to get married. We're definitely not. We're not even engaged. We're just going steady. But am I ever looking forward to Bermuda. I haven't taken a break from my practice in three years. Joan-e says if two people can't find love in Bermuda, forget looking anywhere else in our solar system. But we aren't going there for love, just for sun and fun."

"Going steady? Aren't the two of you … um … a little … Don't answer. Sorry. It's an obvious question. None of my business really. Don't mind me. I suffer from excessive curiosity. Have all my life."

"I like that. Zyg told me you ask a lot of questions. He said it helped a lot on the WestInvest deal."

"Sometimes it helps. Sometimes it gets you into trouble."

"Well, in my experience the only thing most of you Street people stop to question is the size of your paycheques."

"What makes you say that?"

"Well, an example I use with Zyg is you never hear you guys question something as stupid as the idea that shareholders are the only people on the planet who matter. Shareholders? Excuse me. How about secretaries, shipping clerks, and maintenance staff who, after years of dedication, end up jobless while some overpaid wheeler-dealer gets to laugh all the way to the bank, most likely the bank he works for? I mean, how dedicated to your job would you be if you thought the company was going to get sold right from under you three-quarters of the way through your working career? And for what reason? To make some wheeler-dealer and a bunch of shareholders a few extra bucks? Shareholders first. People second. One of the modern world's best-marketed delusions – right up there with our notion of love, wouldn't you say?"

Before I could reply, Jimmy's brother brought our drinks. In the background, I heard: *Fly me to the moon and let me play among the stars ...*

"Mmm, yumm!" Antoinette murmured. "One sip and the world softens right up."

"Up there with love? Yes, Zyg did tell me you have some reservations about it."

"Quite a few, actually. At this point in my life all I need is love to flash another 'user error' in my face. No thanks. Zyg's very kind to me, I have to admit. Very kind. Bermuda's just an example. With what's going on in his office these days, he shouldn't be going anywhere. But he insisted I needed a break. And I had no idea how worn down I was. Didn't even get a honeymoon on my last shot at love."

"Well, I'd say Zyg's wants you to take another – your expression – shot at love. And he's not the least bit ashamed to tell anybody who'll listen."

"Well, one reservation is, with you Street guys, it's always hard to tell exactly what it is you're in love with. Zyg's in love with his job and playing Bay Street Bingo, no question. As to exactly what else he's in love with, could be me, could be with Zygmunt Adams. Or the attraction of another conquest. Joan-e warned me. Our friend Zyg doesn't have a good track record. You have to admit that a man who's a confirmed woman chaser, drives a flashy car, and has an addiction to the racetrack isn't a top-quartile prospect for enduring love. Those aren't the characteristics of a man ready to settle down. And any experienced Bay Street Bingo Player will tell you – poor past performance tends to repeat itself. I'm very fond of Zyg. Please don't get me wrong about that, but his past could be – your expression – a very good leading indicator …"

"I don't see that. I don't want to sound like an attorney for the defence, especially in a debate with a highly skilled barrister, but he does adore you. Even Joan-e, if she were here, would tell you that. And people do change."

"Seen any spotless leopards lately? That's what I say to Zyg. At his age it's too late for spot remover. Whenever Zyg starts to talk about love, I tell him you're just throwing words around. I tell him, you wouldn't know what love was about if you sat through a lecture series put on by the Twelve Apostles. I mean, surely to God he would have found somebody by now. It's not like he's a stay-at-home mom or something. He's out a lot. A lot! On the other hand, I have to admit, he doesn't exactly look like a trophy husband any woman would snap up. But in my business, nothing amazes you. Just today I had a new client – a great-looking guy, a real head-turner, hot, hot, hot – and he told me, 'Like, well, I thought I was in love … two years ago. And now, like, I'm totally not.' Do you think that guy could have had one –" Antoinette bit into her lower lip "– flaming clue what love is about?"

"Zygmunt calls you a philosopher of love. You've read a lot on the subject, he told me."

"A student if anything. From all my reading, I still don't know what love is. People talk about it in such a mixed-up way. What I am, though, is a specialist in un-love. That's my real day job."

"But all you have to do is look at him when he talks about you. I can remember when he bought that horse for you. What did he call her? One Smart Cookie or something? He was so excited you'd think he was in grade school and class was just let out for the summer."

"But, see, he does have a language problem. He called her Biscuit, not Cookie. One Smart Biscuit. He's always getting his expressions mixed up. But, whew, the Biscuit is a beauty. And she and I have the best times together out at FastHorses riding around while Zyg sits through his meetings with Lance and His Worship. For another thing, though, I don't take much hope frankly from the way he dumped his last lady, Big Pharma. Barely gave her enough time to pack her bags and ... and he let her run off with my dog. My goddamn dog!"

Antoinette smiled, and with a shake of her head, tossed a lock of hair from her face, stared into space for a moment, and then turned back. "I don't ask myself – what is love? That's far too complicated. All I want to know is what it is for one adult to love another. You know, the stuff we're supposed to build lasting relationships on. The stuff we get married on. People end up saying things like 'Love is in the air.' That drives me wild. They might as well claim it's in the water, as if love is some kind of physical force like gravity or magnetism. Or worse, a mystical force like voodoo. I think if you want to understand love, you need to make the idea human. It would be much easier if we talked about loving. Loving is something you can see going on. Loving is love in action, not some airy-fairy idea from a movie or a monastery."

My BlackBerry buzzed. "Might be Zyg," I said, taking the device out of my pocket and looking at the screen: "flight cancelled. airport a zoo. taking overnight train back. wish a. happy happy birthday for me. Z." I showed Antoinette what Zyg had written, then typed a reply: "Talk tomorrow. Get home safely. A. and Ferdie."

"Looks like the party isn't going to get off the ground," I said. "Better get you home."

"We have to eat somewhere. Might as well be here. You Bay Street guys are always looking for a free lunch. How about a free dinner? We'll have Jimmy's brother put it on Zyg's tab."

"Here's the deal then," I said. "I buy dinner and you tell me where love's gone off the tracks."

"Zyg and I had a long discussion like that in New York once."

"How'd it work out?"

"We didn't speak for a year. One good thing about it, though, at least when I went out, I could wear my high heels."

Antoinette ordered the Shrimps Rémy. I ordered the same along with a bottle of Chablis. Jimmy's brother brought the wine to our table, and after the approval ritual, filled our glasses. I toasted Antoinette's good health and Zyg's and having many happy years together, not having one clue – not one flaming clue – that such a toast would be as useless as a voodoo curse.

We talked about many things besides love that night, but I don't remember what we said about those other things. Time seemed to stand still, at least in my memory. And whenever we were interrupted by the busboy clearing away our plates or Jimmy's brother pouring wine or coffee, the background music filled any pause in our conversation.

It's not the pale moon that excites me, that thrills and delights me, oh, no …

"Well," I finally said to get the conversation going again, "probably everybody thinks they know what love is. But, unlike you, we don't do our homework. We probably research a new car or a computer more."

"The first time I thought I was in love, I got hurt so badly I cried for weeks. I thought the world had ended. I had to get help. I honestly thought I wouldn't make it through. There were flurries in between that and the second time. But the second time was worse. I married an American guy. He'd been a U.S. Marine. Taught unarmed combat. At parties he'd show friends some of his tactics. His favourite was the 'monkey elbow' to the solar plexus. I called him the Combatant. That was kind of ironic. He was very soft-spoken. And very charming. You wouldn't think he'd harm a flea. You sure you want to hear all this?"

"That's our deal. What could be better than having a very smart woman educate me on love? Frankly, I'm probably more skeptical about it than you."

"The only smart thing about me is I know I'm never smart enough."

"You can back out if you want."

"Well, with the Combatant I was certain I was in love. We didn't rush into marriage. We were engaged for eighteen months. But one night, when I refused to go along with his career plans, he flipped out and came after me – physically. Whatever I'd felt for the man dissolved in two seconds – no, maybe one. I got the hell out of there. I didn't try to find him help. I didn't try to work things out. I just ran."

She paused, took a sip of wine, and tossed a lock of hair back again. "Sometime afterward I realized I didn't really want to be married to him in the first place. I'd convinced myself I was in love. I was busy buying into the dream. Me who sees fake love every day of the week! When you find out you've been lying to yourself, you know what happens? You lose all faith in your judgment. For me, it was the end of any certainty about anything, and for a long, long time. I don't know what I would have done without Zyg's support. It was rough, really rough." Antoinette raised the wineglass to her lips but didn't drink. She just stared off into space as if tasting a memory.

Walk on by. Walk on by ...

"Sounds like some sort of bad trip," I said.

"Well, it wasn't what I expected. Let's put it that way. And that's where the whole problem starts right there – with expectations. The poets and songwriters, movie producers, and all that ilk – the merchants of love, that's what I call them – get you to believe love is some kind of spiritual WD-40 for unfulfilled souls. But that's not what I see every day.

"Most of the time, in the early going, when somebody says they're in love, all they're really doing is reporting on a neurochemical imbalance – an excess of Vasoprin, oxytocin, dopamine, serotonin, endorphins, adrenaline, whatever. It's a new experience to them. They have no idea what to call it. So they label it love. Label is the key word. Usually, it's fake love with a life expectancy of two years at the most, more usually just a couple of orgasms at best. Somewhere along the line the ardour evaporates and the love-struck proclaimant becomes un-struck and then leaves and continues on his merry way like some ... some insouciant mailman."

I laughed. "Talk about not seeing any spotless leopards. How many insouciant mailmen have you bumped into lately?"

"Okay, okay. But believe me. I see it all the time in my practice.

Some guy makes some significant money for the first time in his life. What's happened is a great chunk of luck landed in his little arena of used trucks, or of mispriced stocks, or software apps. So no reason why he can't get lucky somewhere else.

"One guy owned a Toyota dealership. When he courted his wife, nothing was too good for her. Whatever she wanted she got – jewellery, trips to New York, dresses from Chanel or Dior. She could be late, she could change her mind, she could cancel. Didn't matter. He was her slave – right up until his dealership started to make real money. Then overnight he chameleoned – if there's such a word – into the CEO of the household and tried to make her into an executive assistant. He was now the master. Right out of Sartre, I swear. Happens more often than you'd think. Once a guy like that gets rich, he starts thinking he must be smart. Doesn't figure, does it? I mean, a lot of smart people never make big money and a lot of really less-than-smart people, like Cliffy Sutton, who barely got out of grade ten, make piles."

"Antoinette, geez, lady, that's not what Zyg's about. Surely to God …"

"Most of the time what you actually get from the love proclaimant and what you thought you were going to get – most of the time, I'm not saying always – are about as far apart as January and November. I mean, how much farther apart can you get? What else explains the divorce rate? Instead of accepting what someone claims, you'd be better off flipping a coin. Love is a high-risk business at best. The odds aren't in its favour. But the merchants of love don't tell you that. Why? Because that won't help sell their merchandise. Zyg, he likes to play the odds. Me, I've never bought even a $2 lottery ticket in my whole life."

"What you're saying is that Zyg's willing to take a chance, and if it works out, it works out, and if it doesn't, it doesn't?"

"No, Ferdie, all I'm claiming is we've got the whole notion of love totally screwed up these days. It's not some sort of WD-40 for the soul. That's a total delusion. Very often love isn't the end of your worries. It's just the start. The merchants of love have been conning us for hundreds of years, maybe longer."

"Well, let me ask you this. If love ends up in utter disappointment so often, where did it get its great reputation from?"

"As anybody being interviewed on TV and has an answer ready replies, 'Great question.'"

"And the answer is?"

"Branding. One of the great branding jobs of all time. Same tricks they use to get you to believe you can find happiness in a bottle of Coke or self-worth at the wheel of a snazzy SUV, or that the folks over at Cliffy Sutton's boiler shop can make your retirement dreams come true."

"But who did the branding?"

"The merchants of love – the storytellers, poets, songwriters, and the like. Not the preachers. They talk about an entirely different kind of love – God's love. The love I'm talking about is between two adults. Probably the troubadours back in the Middle Ages were the first. They stole the idea from the priests … obviously. But they had one big problem. Where were they going to find someone to endorse their new idea of love with a name as iconic as God's? Where on earth? So they threw in a magic ingredient – sex. At first, not necessarily touchy-feely sex, more just idealized sex. But don't kid yourself, sex nonetheless. Big, big mistake, by the way. Nobody's been able to sort the two out ever since.

"Of course, in those days they only had word-of-mouth marketing. So they put together songs and poems and stories. Took a while, but eventually the brand swept the Western world. And, probably, back in the early, early days added a nice biblical touch by claiming that their new idea of love was the greatest thing since unleavened bread. But nobody fooled old La Rochefoucauld. Back in the 1600s he wrote: 'People would never fall in love if they hadn't heard love talked about.'"

Antoinette deepened her voice. "'Feel more alive. Get with the program. Give your petty little existence a shot of meaningfulness.' All the old tried-and-true tricks branding artists use to manipulate our expectations nowadays."

"Why would anyone fall for it?"

"Makes life so much easier. No need to think things through." The half smile returned to Antoinette's face. "You're the best listener I've had in years. Not often I come across somebody who'll let me blabber on. Want to quit? You can, but let me tell you, I'm having the best time."

"Course not. Could be a breakthrough in human understanding tonight, right here at Thrace's."

The busboy twisted a pepper shaker over our shrimps rather inattentively and refilled our wineglasses.

I'm in the mood for love. Simply because ...

I was beginning to feel on the wrong side of an argument with Socrates or Athena. I knew I was no match for Antoinette. But somebody had to make Zyg's case. I thought my best chance was to lie low and wait for an opening.

"Yummy. Shrimps are delicious. Perfect. I thought I saw a couple of tears of boredom, Ferdie. A lovely white wine and shrimps and a little idle chatter. What could be more fun? But tell me to stop. I can go on, but it wouldn't be worth it if you and I ended up not speaking for the next year."

"I'm fascinated. Outside of funerals and televangelists you don't hear somebody talk about the idea of love."

"Well, my point is that the branding job has been so complete all you have to murmur today is 'love,' and as you Bingo Players like to say, people will back up the truck. I mean, originally you had to slay a dragon or half a dozen infidels to show you meant what you said. But the songwriters and the book writers and all the other word shamans tell you: 'Go ahead. Jump right in. You'll have the time of your life. No commitment needed. Just say the word. That's all you have to do.'

"There's a plaque on Zyg's bathroom wall that declares he was a member of Cliffy Sutton's Circle of the Constantly Committed to the Care of and Concern for the Client. You believe that a slobbering deadbeat like Cliffy Sutton who, I'm told, gave all of $100 to the United Way last year, could come up with something as beautiful as that? My point is – without the care and concern it isn't love.

"Those stupid ads of Cliffy's in *The Community Crier* promising you lifelong security. Will it be Hawaii or the Himalayas? You bet." Antoinette deepened her voice and put the back of her hand beside her mouth. "*Psstt*, like a little security, my friend? *Psstt*, put your life savings with Cliffy Sutton and you'll be able to retire to some cozy condo in downtown Kathmandu or in a charming little beach hut on Oahu."

161

"What's all that got to do with Zyg?"

"Cliffy Sutton taught him the business, for God's sake."

"Are you saying Zyg wouldn't hesitate to sell you a bill of goods any more than Cliffy Sutton would?"

"No, you're missing my point. My point is that Cliffy Sutton is just following the Bay Street crowd without questioning what he's doing. Maybe Zyg's doing the same thing. One thing I do know is that the last thing I need in my life is another tsunami of disappointment."

"Well, I can tell you what he thinks he's doing," I interjected. "You might not agree. But he thinks he's showing you, trite as it might sound, what he's really about, that he's not one of those Bay Street sex-and-money guys, the only kind of *Homo sapiens* you think exists on Bay Street. He's trying to run an IED dedicated to care and respect for the people who work there and for the people they do business with. And when I ask why he wants to do that, he answers – I swear – he's doing it, as far-fetched as this might sound, mostly to prove to one Antoinette Mairie that he's not out to exploit anyone, though he openly admits his past might suggest otherwise. That's why he wanted you at the awards dinner so badly – to hear what the industry had to say about him." There was a pause, and I thought for a moment I'd made Zyg's case.

Smile while your heart is breaking ...

"You make me sound heartless," Antoinette finally said. "Look, I'd be blind not to see he's a bit smitten. But, you know, Zyg told me he was engaged before he pulled up stakes and came to Canada. And that kind of experience can turn someone into a serial womanizer for life. Another thing, he never talks about his mother, never. I wonder in his past whether somebody or some situations – you know, a bunch of rejections, betrayals, even his own misunderstandings – might have crushed his ability to really care for someone else. People jump to the wrong idea about love all the time. 'Dad obviously loved you more. That's why he left you more – not because you'll be in a wheelchair for the rest of your life.' If you're a lawyer, you see that kind of stuff all the time."

"Are you saying Zyg's not capable of love?"

"Maybe, maybe not. My point is it's not easy for anybody to sort it out these days. Even neuroscientists are confused. They think love is nothing more than an emotion. Love involves feelings and emotions, obviously, but that's only part of the story. For me, being in love is a way of experiencing the world, a way of being, if that's not too airy-fairy. The neuro-folks think they can scan love with their fMRIs. I say no matter how much they like to spy on the brain, they'll never see a broken heart any more than ophthalmologists rummaging around our eyeballs will find our souls. And who volunteers for these experiments? Students who don't have one flaming clue about love. And that raises the question whether a grown man with a fancy Porsche who plays the ponies big-time and runs an ongoing Bingo operation would understand love any better than a clueless student."

"You can't be serious. People change. Do you talk to Zyg like this?"

"When I can get him to sit still long enough."

"You know anybody you'd claim without question was in love?"

"Yes, my aunt and uncle. I'm not saying it's impossible. I'm just saying it's much rarer than people think. A lot rarer, and much, much quieter. And it takes a large chunk of time to find out whether both participants have gotten out of the launch stage and made it into orbit where there's a constant commitment to the care and concern."

"Come on, isn't the kind of love you're talking about something a person recognizes spontaneously like beauty?"

That's exactly what the branding artists want you to think. They want you to think that surge of emotion signifies a lasting commitment to the care and concern of the human being in play. It doesn't. We know that. Most of the time all that caring and concern fizzles out in short order for one reason or another. Humans are no good at predicting. Why would we be good at predicting at first sight what our feelings will be a year or fifty years from that moment? Sure, sometimes some people get it right. Just like the Bingo Players who predict the market. They get it right sometimes. But it's more likely a matter of luck than anything."

"You've lost me."

Let me go back. It's the branders, the merchants of love, the story-tellers who throw us off. They like to describe the 'customer experience' of love. But love isn't a story. Love isn't Romeo and Juliet. That's a story, a very good one, but a story nonetheless. They only knew each other for less than a week. Love isn't a story. Stories make sense. Life doesn't. That's where religion got into the act, by the way. You can't see love. You can only see 'loving' – the care and concern at work, for example. My aunt and uncle fight and argue all the time, especially when they lose at bridge. But beneath all that you can see in the way he mixes her a martini or gets her coffee in the morning a magnificent sense of devotion. Hard as you look, you'll never see devotion floating around in the air like the fog outside tonight."

"Okay, but look. We wouldn't get out of bed in the morning if we had to have a thorough understanding of everything we said or did all day. You're asking too much of everybody, not just Zyg."

And so we bantered back and forth for most of the evening until Jimmy's brother came over and said, "No hurry, Mr. Swasont, but we'd like to close up."

Antoinette and I were the only diners left.

I paid the bill, though Antoinette favoured making Zyg pay. It started to rain heavily as I drove to her place.

"I'd ask you up for a nightcap, but I'm truly dead tired," she told me. "Just let me off at the front door. No use both of us getting wet. Thank you for a lovely evening."

I took one final stab for Zyg. "I think you can see love if you look closely. When you're in Bermuda and relaxed a bit with all that sun and sea, take a close look at Zyg. You'll see it in his eyes, in his gestures, in that smug look he has on his face when he's around you. There's loving going on. You'll see it."

For the first time that evening, Antoinette conceded ground. "You really believe that?"

"No question. Absolutely no question in my mind. He's totally committed to you. Otherwise he wouldn't still be around."

"Really?"

"No question!"

"Really?"

"Really!"

"Jesus."

13
Best-Laid Plans

Sent: 27/04/2007 12:27 a.m.
To: hmarkson2177@gmail.com
From: zygadams1@yahoo.ca
Subject: Change in Plans
Status: URGENT

harv, am in air canada lounge at airport with laptop. tried phone u today many times. no luck. turns out i need a little heart procedure in Germany (too slow here – long story). arranged by my doctor aunt from frankfurt (gadambrowski@kgu.de). she told me to come today – cancellation. cant visit u tomorrow. SORRY. SORRY. SORRY. no choice. believe me. will contact u when up & around.

IMPORTANT: TELLING EVERYBODY HERE MEETING WITH GOTT MOVED UP (REALLY NOT). CANT TELL ANTOINETTE. SHE WOULD TRY TO TALK ME OUT OF IT.

havent been able to make contact with her. when antoinette mairie hears this she will want my head on a platter. If she's not successful, will resched soon, very soon.

best to you and katherine the ingrate.

sorry. sorry. sorry.

Z.

Sent from my BlackBerry.

Some days technology is a boon and other days it definitely isn't. Zyg couldn't get through to Antoinette until late afternoon just before the last call for boarding his flight. And I was at a cocktail party with

165

Joan-e and the Testosteros and out to dinner after. I didn't get home until well after midnight. I wasn't expecting any voice mail, so I didn't pick up my mesessage until the next morning:

"Ferdy, I'm calling from the plane just about to taxi out for takeoff and don't have time to text you. I have another reason for taking this flight and haven't got time to go into it. I told Antoinette I had to change the meeting date with that guy in Frankfurt I told you about, Gott de Holger, the guy I told you who could make or break IED's plans for Europe. That meant cancelling Bermuda. Only got through to her a couple of minutes ago. She was at some goddamn new hairdresser's all afternoon.

I told Antoinette it's my only chance to meet with de Holger. Everything depends on me to get Europe going. All she said was 'I understand. I'm deeply disappointed, but not surprised.' I didn't like the sound of her voice. Soft. Very soft and very compliant. That's not my Antoinette.

I'm not cancelling, I told her. Just postponing. We'll go later. No question. I promise. Cross my heart, I said. Cross my heart and hope ... she didn't hear me. She'd hung up. I tried to phone her back. No go. Probably took the phone off the hook.

I'm really worried. Please call her and kind of cool her out. I'll be back in a week. Thanks, Ferdy. Thanks. I'll be in touch as soon as I can and explain it all. I'll be bringing you a big bottle of the best Scotch they have in the duty-free."

Cross Bennett, a few weeks later, admitted to me that when he first heard about what happened to Zyg, he thought there had been some kind of accident on the autobahn.

■ ■ ■

I phoned Dr. Biranya, the consulting cardiologist at ExecuMed Heath Services (which my brother and I had used for years), and he invited me to come over to his office at University Hospital that afternoon.

He was a very formal man, dressed in a three-piece suit and a conservative blue-striped tie. With old-world courtesy, he held the door open as he showed me into his office and then made sure I was comfortable in the chair beside his desk. His office reminded me of Kopsin's. The walls were covered – plastered – with degrees, diplomas, certificates, but instead of charts, there were diagrams of the heart from every angle with this affliction or that (though not one of the broken or lost variety, nor a picture of the kind of heart one needs to carry on). For the first few minutes, he said nothing, just shuffled through papers in a manila folder, then typed on his keyboard and squinted at the monitor in front of him.

The doctor cleared his throat. "Zygmunt told me during his annual checkup that he'd been too busy the past few months to work out and the only change he noticed was a shortness of breath when he took the stairs up to his office. And of late a few chest pains. But after the results came back from the angiogram I insisted he take, I told him he needed open-heart surgery to replace his aortic valve, and that frankly, I didn't understand why he didn't have more severe symptoms. He asked me how long he would be out of action, and I told him six weeks.

"He said he was much too busy to take that much time off and asked if I couldn't give him some sort of pills to tide him over. When I told him there were no pills that would do that, he asked if there was some quicker solution at some place like the Mayo Clinic. I said no, not in North America, but there were some hospitals in Europe that performed a procedure called a TAVI, using a catheter instead of open-heart surgery. But I said it wouldn't likely be approved in North America for another four or five years. They claimed the recovery time was a matter of a few days rather than weeks. Zygmunt wanted to know what the downside was. I told him their studies indicated a mortality rate of about 3 percent. He said that was odds of thirty-three to one in his favour and that he hadn't had odds like that since his weekly squash opponent had left for Bermuda. After that we never spoke again."

Zyg must have phoned his doctor aunt in Frankfurt. Within a day, evidently, she arranged for a hospital in Leipzig to accept him. The doctors there had pioneered the procedure and had performed it dozens and dozens of times, though usually on patients much older than Zyg and not in as good health.

■ ■ ■

A small black-bordered announcement appeared in *The World of Finance* :

It is with great sadness that IED Securities Inc. has to announce that it has lost its courageous leader, Zygmunt Adams, to an unsuccessful heart operation performed in Leipzig, Germany, last week.

Mr. Adams specifically requested that neither a funeral nor a memorial service be held. The many members of the staff and of the clubs he belonged to and his many other friends will miss his exuberance, dedication, and sense of humour. They are asked to spend a moment in silence at their own convenience. Any memorial donations should be made to:

Horsemen's Protective Society
Box 121, 444 Rexdale Blvd.
Toronto, Ontario M9W 3L1

 IED SECURITIES

STABILITY.
INTEGRITY.
COMPACTNESS.

A week later, in the Tuesday, May 8, 2007, edition of *The World of Finance*, this appeared:

HALVERT TULVIN
Goings-On
htulvin@worldoffinance.ca

NEW EXECS FOR IED

Sherwin Chable, chairman of the board of IED Securities Inc., announced today the appointment of Mr. W. Cross Bennett of Winnipeg, Manitoba, as chief executive officer and Mr. Charles "Chicky" Glickerman of Toronto as president and chief operating officer. These changes were brought about by the unexpected and untimely passing two weeks ago of the late Zygmunt Adams, the former chief executive and chief operating officer.

IED had been struggling in late 2003. And though the company was shopped around The Street, nobody showed the slightest interest in buying it. That's when Mr. Adams came on board. Almost from the day he joined the company its fortunes changed, and it began a meteoric rise to become the sixth-largest wealth management firm in Canada and by far the fastest growing. The financial industry named him Wealth Management Executive of the Year for 2006 in recognition of his achievement and what he called his people-first business model.

"Much of that," according to Toddy Landau, a close associate of Mr. Adams, "was due to his determination to revolutionize the way the wealth management industry did business. If you put many financial service companies under a microscope, you'll find, in spite of all their talk and advertising to the contrary, the clients' needs seldom come before those of the company's, its executives', or its advisers'. The first thing he did as CEO was to do away with quotas. Then he literally turned the company on its head: the name for registered representatives was changed to account executives, whose job it was to keep the clients happy, no longer to present predictions about the future price of this or that stock."

Perhaps one of his best moves was to hire away from Sutton Securities Kopsin Shurtz as the chief investment officer. Mr. Shurtz seems to have an almost encyclopedic knowledge of markets. It was his responsibility to design the template for each client's account and manage the investments while the account executive's job was to coordinate whatever resources for his financial well-being the client needed, from legal to tax planning.

"People around IED didn't think much of the idea at first," Mr. Landau remarked. "Many, I'm sure, would have left had the markets looked a little healthier. Most went along because they had no choice. Fortunately, the markets began to rise. Morale picked up. And soon discontented clients from other brokerage houses were getting the message – all word of mouth – and the referrals started rolling in."

"The key, "according to Sky Czsymarka [sic], head of research and an eleven-year veteran with the firm, "was that Zyg cared to an unusual degree about the people, whether clients or employees. Every complaint or suggestion from a client went across his desk. Zyg's unceasing optimism and Shurtz's understanding of markets won clients, staff, and partners over. If a mistake was made or an error occurred or the client's intentions were misinterpreted, the situation was given urgency and rectified at the company's cost immediately."

Mr. Adams was forty-seven years old. In his will, he requested no funeral or memorial service be held. Sources said his ashes were strewn on his grandfather's farm in his hometown of Freblis, Germany.

In a phone conversation, Mr. Chable, who resides in Panama City, Panama, said the board of directors had decided to change the firm's name to IED Wealth and Well-Being Management Group and to create new opportunities for growth by reinstituting investment banking and making IPOs available again to clients.

"Our commitment," he said, "to deliver excellence in research, trading, and customer service won't change. We have no plans to rebrand ourselves. In Mr. Bennett and Mr. Glickerman, we have two men with a long history of service excellence. That just shows the resources a vibrant company like ours has at its fingertips."

In a way, Antoinette saved herself from all that.

14
Splinters of Hope

Within view of the Old City Hall's clock tower, shortly after midnight, Zyg's flight not yet landed in Frankfurt, a blue Volvo swerved off the Gardiner Expressway onto the off ramp – as if the driver had taken notice too late – and splintered into a thousand pieces the large green sign with white lettering that proudly announced Bay Street below.

The body was buried in the family plot in Saint-Gabriel-de-Brandon, Quebec, next to the grave of her father, who had succumbed years before to a staph infection (methicillin-resistant *Staphylococcus aureus*) contracted while in hospital for a broken hip, and next to that of a younger sister who had died in infancy.

Two weeks later a memorial service sponsored by Joan-e took place at The Elm Tree. The parking garage filled up early, and some people had to park blocks away. Only Joan-e spoke, and at that only briefly.

"I doubt the great poets or even the finest preachers could find words that would come anywhere close to describing the wound I feel and perhaps you feel. Nor do I for one second understand why this happened." Joan-e lifted her head. "Nor, my sweet friend, do I have any idea where you are or where you're on your way to. Wherever that is, my sweet-faced, sweet, sweet friend, safe journey."

According to Antoinette's aunt, everything – the clothes, furniture, books, proceeds from the sale of her condo, and her investments – went to an organization promoting women's rights, as the will designated.

Everything except a gold ring found on the living room floor. That was sent on to her mother in England as a keepsake.

■ ■ ■

In October that year the market, as measured by the Dow Jones Index, hit its highest point in history. By that time, Kopsin and his new wife had passed through the Panama Canal on their one-hundred-and-eleven-day world cruise. Kopsin responded from Apia, Samoa, to my email. He wrote that he had been called into the Grand Ballroom one Friday afternoon in early August and was told that his negative attitude toward the market over the past year was destroying IED. Cross Bennett told him clients had forgone millions and millions in profits over the previous months as the market rose, contrary to Kopsin's prediction. The new executive felt, according to Cross, that Kopsin had lost either his faith in the markets or his understanding of them. On the other hand, IED had built itself by holding, through thick and thin, a "constructive" attitude toward the markets.

IED never did get to add "International" to its name. No sooner was Kopsin out the door (actually docking in Kota Kinabalu on the northwest coast of Borneo) than the turbulence began in the fall of 2007 – and it wasn't neurochemical turbulence. As the great Hyman Minsky is said to have observed, the good times don't roll on forever. Over the following eighteen months, the market dropped, hiccupped back up, then plunged as the banking world blew up. And, of course, so did IED, as Cross had so uncannily foreseen in the very first days of the Zyg Adams regime.

The Chables, of course, wanted no part of recessionary times (what good was a tax loss to them?). They convinced their partners that the best way out was to sell even if they all got very little for the shares they still held. The sole bidder was the Federal Wealth and Great Trust division of the Federal Financial Group of Canada.

IED account executives got new business cards with their designations changed back to "financial adviser" (though around the office they were still called "reps"), and where advantageous for marketing reasons, were awarded vice-presidential titles. And quotas were reintroduced,

171

sales pitches were honed, and new issues of stock were hustled out the door like fresh produce on a busy day down at the city food terminal.

■ ■ ■

The provincial regulator put together a team of psychologists, sociologists, neuroscientists, forensic accounts, and four lawyers to try to get a better understanding of the Mormon Knee Affliction (though with a much longer and more official-sounding name). Early on in its work, the team concluded that the disease was embedded in the genetic makeup of the big banks and at that present time there was no known cure. Emboldened by that discovery, the lawyers decided to form a partnership and left for a much higher-paying assignment. The study was then abandoned shortly after that, not halfway through its mandate.

Once so full of life and laughter, the fourth floor of 370 Bay lay empty, still, and silent as a corpse. A block north the clock in the tower of Old City Hall peered down lower Bay Street indifferently as if nothing momentous had happened at IED, as if it never had any hope that The Street would change its ways.

But last year Toddy Landau's son, Teddy, and a fellow adviser known around the office as "H.R." (from his time as a professional baseball pitcher with the Baltimore Orioles) got fed up with Federal Wealth and Great Trust. They left and started a boutique firm. When young Teddy discovered that H.R.'s first name was Hugh, he insisted their company be called "Hugh R. Furst Investor Services" and based it on Zyg's model for a service organization.

A letter appeared in one of Toby Williams's recent "Frequently Unanswered Questions" columns in *Today's Business*:

> Toby, here's a simple solution to advisers acting in the best interest of their clients − the so-called problem of "fiduciary duty." Why don't financial advisers who do act in that way make it known? That's the first thing we do.
>
> On all our printed material, in our legal agreements, and on our website, we say: "Please be aware that we proudly assume full legal responsibility *to act in the best interests of our clients at all times*. If, for any reason, you feel we have not done so in your case, email help@ombudsman.on.org. And be assured of our full co-operation as well as our willingness to assume all costs to remedy the situation if in any way at all we violated that policy."

That would save a heck of a lot of muss and fuss. It would eliminate all ambiguity. No new set of regulations would be needed. Only those advisers and reps [and producers] who wanted to would deploy such notice voluntarily. Everybody else need only refrain. What could be simpler?

Theodore Landau, President
Hugh R. Furst Investor Services
Toronto, Canada

Besides Teddy's efforts, there's another valid reason for optimism: remember how Antoinette used to tease Zyg with "Seen any spotless leopards lately?" whenever he claimed he'd changed his ways? And how she called him "Spots" to remind him? Well, she was wrong. Flat wrong. Just the other day an article appeared on the second page of *The World of Finance* that claimed: roaming the grasslands of Botswana, several members of a species of spotless leopard had been seen (spotted).

Epilogue:

Loose Ends, Unfinished Business, Et Cetera

However attractive Zyg found the odds of thirty-three to one in his favour when he chose to undergo the heart procedure in Leipzig, he knew only too well that every bet has two sides.

The day before he got the call from his aunt to rush over to Europe, his (and Harvey's) lawyer, Gordie Elliott, was out of town as usual when needed most (in Oaxaca this time). So Zyg wrote out a will by hand himself – a holographic will. He then had it witnessed by his executive assistant, though evidently that wasn't required to be legally binding.

Next, Zyg made three photocopies: one for his own records, two he put in regular envelopes on which he scribbled: "Do not open unless necessary." One was destined for Bermuda by FedEx, the other was to be sent to me by regular mail. The original he had couriered to Gordie's office.

The will stated that in case one day Harvey did decide to return to Toronto he would receive Zyg's BlackBerry (password: zyg777) with the phone numbers of all of Zyg's past female acquaintances (who knows how many megabytes that took up?). The will also bequeathed $50,000 to pay off the mortgage of Mrs. Avagadro, the lady who came in each week to clean and restore order to Admiral Crescent, as thanks for her help over the years and all the sound advice given. (Although, the will admitted, not all of it was taken.) Those were the only two defined bequests. Everything else was left to Antoinette. It took months to settle the estate.

Along with the other IED shareholders, Zyg's estate ended up selling its shares to Federal Wealth and Great Trust for next to nothing in late 2008. The shares Zyg held in other enterprises such as the $184,000 in Save Your Time Software Inc. had next to no value. The proceeds from the sale of his shares in Pluman's Funeral Homes helped to cover Gordie Elliott's outsized legal bills. The will did specify no funeral or memorial service but expressed regret at not taking advantage of Pluman's discount for shareholders.

As far as taxes were concerned, the capital losses more than offset any gains. After all the other expenses such as paying off the home-equity loan, the real-estate commission, and the provincial and new municipal land transfer taxes on the sale of Admiral Crescent, there wasn't that much left, really, except for the shares of FastHorses Inc. By provincial law, whatever was left of Zyg's estate after the stated bequests were fulfilled – or could not be fulfilled – was to go to his closest living relative, in this case his mother in Hamburg, a woman with a shrewdness not passed on to her son. Gordie had to get three different appraisals of Zyg's interest in FastHorses before she consented to sell the shares.

Why in the world I bought them, I have had great difficulty figuring out. Though I did a lot of horseback riding at summer camp in my teens, I never had a great interest in horse racing, much less in horse breeding.

Shortly after Cross returned to Toronto and took over IED, I met with him in the Grand Ballroom. He was not the least bit sympathetic to Zyg's fate. In great detail, with no sign of compassion, he told me about his reaction when he first read the email that announced Zyg as the new president of IED. And in equal detail he described his conversation with his stepfather/lawyer.

Cross felt Toronto had double-crossed him. It should have made him CEO when it was decided to give Big Bobby "The Shaft." He maintained that every innovation, every new policy, and every change introduced by Zyg had taken IED in the wrong direction completely, the sole exception being the idea to start a sales operation in Europe, since the timing was so right. And, in his opinion, investing in a horse farm showed how little business sense Zyg had.

"Zyg thought we could remove all the conflicts of interest," Cross said, strutting around his offices as if on a victory lap. "You can't. Somebody has to be better off and somebody worse off with every trade, simple as that. It's a mistake on one party's part and a gain for the other.

"I tried to tell him we wouldn't make a bloody nickel in the bond business if we made our prices public. Once you do that, clients shop. And that's the end of any profit. Most don't even know they're getting a haircut. Why stir things up? One way or another IED has to get paid. But Zyg wouldn't listen. Instead of just waiting patiently in 2003 for the market to come back, he had this stupid idea that we needed to change the way we did business. 'Becoming professional,' he called it. Or 'eliminating the *caveat emptor.*' Sometimes he talked as if he was trying to save The Street from itself. I couldn't stop him, God knows. But I could put my foot in the spokes every chance I got."

Zyg wouldn't be the first person in history to introduce a new way of doing things only to get hung up by a Cross, believe me.

So when I agreed to buy Zyg's shares of FastHorses I thought at the time it was to show Cross how I felt about Zyg as my friend and what he stood for. Lance and His Worship knew horses, Zyg complained more than once, but they didn't have a clue about balance sheets and cash flow. I knew FastHorses couldn't survive without constant financial oversight.

Over the next two years, FastHorses grew from twelve horses to sixty and from just two employees to nine. This year a pair of two-year-olds has shown all kinds of speed. In her second race, a two-furlong dash, Fast Potatoes (out of Velocity Velma by Steak Frites) equalled the track record of 20.91 seconds. And there's Fast Otto, a handsome chestnut colt His Worship swears can accelerate out of the gate faster than any two-year-old he's ever seen, though it's no easy task to get him in the gate in the first place. Both horses are among the leading contenders for next year's big race, the Queen's Plate, for Canadian-bred three-year-olds.

At a fall auction one of our yearlings fetched the highest price of the evening. We're still far from profitable, but the enterprise has built a reputation for being "smart, fast, and reliable." It would make any branding expert proud. We did it without the usual bag of tricks simply by being smart, fast, and reliable and because that was the only way Lance and His Worship knew how to do business.

■ ■ ■

Only in stories can motives be pinned down neatly. The motives at play in everyday life, I find, are seldom simple or unalloyed. At least I had to acknowledge to myself another reason for involvement with FastHorses. I couldn't help but speculate on what would have happened that Saturday night had I come home to catch Zyg's call. Things would have turned out much differently, I'm convinced. From our conversation at Thrace's, I knew exactly how much Bermuda meant to Antoinette and I knew, too, from that conversation how very, very vulnerable she was. There isn't a single doubt in my mind I would have been down there banging on her door within ten minutes of speaking with Zyg.

Of course, I wouldn't have had the medical facts behind Zyg's change of plans. I couldn't have told her that Zyg was shielding her from getting involved in the hospital process. But I did know from his message there was something unusual that made his change in plans necessary. And I would have insisted that she find out what that was before coming to any conclusions.

Could I have dissuaded her? I'd had some luck at Thrace's pleading Zyg's case. The thought haunted me.

As chief financial officer of FastHorses, I attended the Sunday management meetings with Lance and His Worship. After, I would take Antoinette's horse, Smarty (officially One Smart Biscuit), out on the trails just the way she had. And I would have these imaginary conversations with her. On one ride, I got carried away and said, "I think I'm in love."

"What, Ferdy, you in love?" I imagined her replying. "You catching the Zyg disease? Have you ever had a decent relationship with anybody in your whole life other than that hooker – excuse me, lap dancer – you put through school?" I could picture her throwing her head back to clear a lock from her face, and I could hear her, or so I felt, laughing her mocking laugh. "A guy like you in love? Who could the lucky little lady be?"

"You, Antoinette."

"You, Ferdy? In love with me? You? Oh, good! Just what I need – another Bay Street Bingo Player. You people are far too busy being in love with yourselves to love somebody else."

I had always been wary of entanglements. My father drank a lot, just like Eldred. I could never figure out whether that was the cause or the effect of why he and my mother never got along. Nor did it help when my brother, eight years older, who I had always looked up to, had to get married and enter into a relationship of constant arguments.

Not so long ago, as I was about to go through the useless exercise of trying to find a publisher for this manuscript, something happened, the sort of thing that seems to happen only to storytellers or their protagonists.

Out of the blue, Rachel, the woman I had helped through divinity school, left a message on my home phone. Other than a condolence card with "Sorry to read about Zyg" written above her name, I hadn't heard from her since she had left to take over the parish outside Ottawa.

In keeping with the claim of full, plain, and true disclosure made earlier on, I feel obliged to add what she said word for word (except, for reasons of modesty, excising her comments about our sex life):

"Ferdinand, it's me, Rache. I'm not much on writing as you know. You remember how much I struggled and struggled with my essays back in my university days. What I want to ask you would take me forever to get down on paper.

I'm coming back to Toronto to complete my doctorate. But I've never explained why I left so abruptly.

Though I never said so for various reasons, I'd fallen in love with you.

But after you and Zyg did the WestInvest deal, you started to hang out with him more and more. Knowing his reputation and

*how coldly, in the end, he treated Lizzie-Ann, I was deathly afraid
similar treatment awaited me once I got my doctorate. So I cut
short my studies and took the job in Perth.*

*But all this time I've missed terribly your wonderful
companionship and all that fantastic* [redacted] *...*

*You know how frank and to the point I can be. With all the
things that have happened of late, I was wondering – can I be very
blunt? – if you had any desire to restart our relationship, but this
time as something more than a commercial friendship?"*

In the end ...

About the Author

John D. Frankel received a B.A. from the University of Toronto, a Diplôme d'Étude from the Sorbonne, and an M.A. in philosophy from the University of Waterloo. After that, for the error of his ways, he spent more than forty years in the financial services business, mostly on the fringe.

He likes to think about things.

Acknowledgements

For this author, writing is very much a solo journey, one that would be difficult to get through without help and encouragement. For those, I would like to thank and acknowledge my editors, Victoria White and Michael Carroll; my publishing coordinator, Daniel Crack; my (more than two) friends; and, most of all, Ms. B.A. Simonsen, my wife, for both her unending encouragement and near-infinite tolerance.